CW01499376

Also by Brian Bowyer

For Jamie and the Magician

ROAD HARVEST

by

Brian Bowyer

Chapter 1

Midnight in Los Angeles: a mosaic of light and motion; electric blue and yellow against a starless sky. Traffic swept by in endless streams of headlight glow along the boulevard.

"I wish," Jinx said, on the parked car's passenger side, "that I liked anything as much as you white boys like cocaine."

Leo shoved his compact mirror and straw beneath the driver's seat. "I know plenty of black dudes who like cocaine."

"Shit, not *this* black dude." Jinx took a drink from the bottle of whiskey he was holding.

Leo started the engine and put the car back on the road.

The night was warm. They rode with their windows down. The air reeked of ozone and monoxides.

"Did you remember to feed Victor?" Leo said.

"Nah, man. I forgot."

"We'd better pick him up something to eat."

Jinx pointed straight ahead. "There's a Burger Joint."

"You think he'll eat Burger Joint?"

"Shit, man. Victor will eat anything."

Leo pulled up to the menu at the drive-through.

"Welcome to Burger Joint. May I take your order, please?"

"Just a second." Leo turned to Jinx. "What should we get him?"

"Just get him like ten hamburgers, or something."

Leo turned back to the menu. "Okay."

There was no response from the menu.

"I'm ready to order."

Again, there was no response.

A man in line behind them yelled, "Hurry up, asshole!"

Leo and Jinx looked at each other.

"That motherfucker just called you an asshole," Jinx said.

Leo nodded. "I heard him."

He got out and approached a truck in line behind them.

In the truck, a fat man sat behind the steering wheel, eating a candy bar. His window was down. Otherwise, the truck was empty.

Leo lit a cigarette. "Were you talking to me?"

"Damn right. I don't have all night."

Leo took a puff off his cigarette. "Step out of the truck, please."

The fat man took a bite of his candy bar.

Leo jammed the lit end of his cigarette into the fat man's forehead. Then he yanked the door open and pulled him out of the truck. From the holster beneath his jacket, he retrieved his gun and started pistol-whipping the man's face.

A different voice from the menu: *"Are you ready to order yet?"*

Still in the car, Jinx leaned over across the driver's side. "Not yet."

Leo dragged the bleeding man to the back of the Cadillac. "Pop the trunk."

Jinx popped open the trunk, but Leo couldn't lift the man by himself. "I need some help. The son of a bitch is too heavy."

Jinx got out and kicked the man in the face a couple of times. Then they wrangled him off the ground and stuffed him inside the trunk.

They left.

Chapter 2

Victor greeted them in the driveway. His tail was wagging, but he didn't bark.

They got out.

Jinx opened a fast-food bag. He started unwrapping hamburgers and dropping them on the ground. "There you go, Victor."

The massive Rottweiler immediately began to feed.

Leo opened the trunk, and Jinx helped him get their hostage out. Then the fat man crashed onto the ground.

"Stand up," Leo told him.

The fat man stood up. One of his eyes had swollen shut. He was still bleeding from his broken nose and several cuts on his forehead and face. His lips were split, and he was missing a couple of teeth. "What the fuck is wrong with you guys?"

"There's not a damned thing wrong with us," Jinx said. "But there's a whole lot wrong with you. You should have kept your mouth shut long enough for my man here to place a fucking order."

"Look, I'm sorry. Okay?"

"No," Leo said. "It's not okay. And because you called me an asshole, you're going on a little ride with us."

"A ride? To where? What are you talking about?"

Leo retrieved a roll of duct tape from his jacket. "If you had just kept your mouth shut long enough to finish your candy bar, you would be wherever you were going. However, since you couldn't eat with your mouth shut, now you're never going to eat again."

"You're going to starve me?"

"No, but you're going on a ride with us, and we don't allow food in the bus."

"Look, mister, please—"

Leo taped his mouth shut.

The man continued to mumble, but stopped when Jinx drew a pistol and aimed it at his face. "Okay, fat man. Into the meat wagon."

They forced him into a barn next to the compound's main house, and Leo turned on some lights. Inside the barn was a silver tour bus, forty-five feet long, with tinted cockpit windows, and a tinted windshield. There were no windows along the sides, or on the back.

They forced him inside the bus and shoved him to the back, where Leo handcuffed him to a steel pole that ran from the floor to the ceiling. "Get used to it, fat man. You'll be here for a while. If you want to sleep, do it. If you need to go to the bathroom, hold it until we ask you if you need to go. And whatever you do, don't make any noise."

Jinx whistled. Seconds later, the Rottweiler joined them in the back. "Victor doesn't like a lot of noise. If you make too much noise, he'll rip your goddamn throat out."

The Rottweiler stared at the fat man. His tail wasn't wagging.

"Victor will watch you tonight," Leo said. "We'll see you in the morning."

They left the bus and walked out of the barn.

While crossing the yard, Jinx said, "He'll suffer without food."

"You think so?"

"Definitely. It's a long ride to the east coast."

Leo shrugged. "He won't starve."

They entered the main house. Each grabbed two suitcases. Then they went upstairs. They walked into a room that featured a table, a vault, and nothing else.

Leo opened the vault. "What all do we need?"

Jinx shrugged. "The usual."

They packed semiautomatic pistols, revolvers, shotguns, assault rifles, plenty of ammo, handcuffs, chains, ropes, a few bombs, and a box of silencers.

Back downstairs, Jinx said, "Let's get a few hours of sleep."

Leo nodded. "See you at dawn."

Chapter 3

The sun was shining, and people swarmed the sidewalks like cockroaches. Tina was easily distracted while she walked, often peering into storefront windows, or examining posters nailed to telephone poles. She received curious glances from the several passersby on foot with whom she nearly collided, and she did her best to return their stares with sinister-looking glares of her own. She enjoyed watching them all shake their heads while they walked away.

Eventually, she reached her destination—a sprawling, single-story brick building with widely spaced windows, a flat roof, and a GREYSTONE MENTAL HEALTH FACILITIES sign in the front parking lot.

She entered the building. The lobby was empty. A receptionist sat behind a desk.

Tina approached the desk.

"May I help you?" the receptionist said.

"I'm here to see Doctor Anderson."

"Do you have an appointment?"

"Yes."

"What's your name?"

"Tina Miller."

"Have you been here before?"

"No."

"Do you have health insurance?"

Tina pulled a card from her purse and gave it to the receptionist. "Just Medicaid. I was told on the phone that you accept Medicaid."

The receptionist gave Tina an ink pen and a clipboard. "Have a seat and fill out these forms while I process your information."

Tina did, and the receptionist returned her Medicaid card when—minutes later—Tina turned in her paperwork.

"Just have a seat again," the receptionist said, smiling. "The doctor will see you soon."

Tina returned to the same chair she had chosen previously. There were several magazines on a table near her chair. She picked one up, flipped through it briefly, and then put it down, struggling to sit still; struggling to stop pulling her own hair; struggling to stop tugging on her earlobes. She got up, walked over to a water fountain, and took a few drinks. Then she splashed some water on her face.

"Tina Miller?" a woman said, behind her.

Tina turned around.

"Doctor Anderson will see you now."

She followed the woman through a door into the back and down a hallway to another door upon which hung a plaque that read DR. MORGAN ANDERSON, PSYCHIATRIST.

The woman opened the door. "You can go on in and have a seat."

Tina stepped into the office.

Doctor Morgan Anderson—a lean, middle-aged white man with thick, slicked-back hair—sat behind his desk. Tina found him handsome for his age.

There were two chairs in front of his desk, and a sofa along the wall to the left. He looked up from some paperwork, and smiled. She thought his teeth were perfect.

"Tina Miller, it's a pleasure to meet you. Please close the door and have a seat."

She closed the door and sat down on the chair nearest the sofa. With her purse slung over a shoulder, she immediately began bouncing a knee and tugging on her earlobes.

"I've gone over your files." He looked down at his papers. "You were diagnosed with bipolar-one disorder at an early age, and borderline personality disorder, and social-anxiety disorder. And in a lot of these notes I'm reading 'borderline schizophrenia.' What made you decide to come and see me?"

"I used to go to Appalachian Mental Health, where Doctor Dyer was my psychiatrist for many years. For most of my life, actually. But then he left, and I got stuck with a bitch named Michelle Blevins. Do you know her?"

He nodded, and gave her a sly smile. "Yes, I know Michelle. She can be rather difficult. I think she has a superiority complex."

"Yes! That's what I think, too! I fucking hate her. I put up with her for a year, but finally I couldn't take her anymore. So I got in the phone book and started calling around, seeing which psychiatrists would take Medicaid. And that's how I found you, Doctor Anderson."

"Please, call me Morgan."

"Are you sure?"

"Absolutely. I want to be your friend, Tina. And I don't want you to feel inferior to me in any way. We all have our problems, believe me."

Tina ran fingers through her hair. "I wish I could smoke in here."

He retrieved an ashtray from a drawer and set it on his desk, close to Tina. "By all means."

She cocked her head. "Are you serious?"

He smiled. "I can keep a secret if you can. Besides, you're my last appointment of the day, and I have plenty of air freshener."

"Okay. If you say so." She retrieved a pack of smokes and a lighter from her purse, and lit a cigarette. She took several long, hard puffs, and then blew a series of smoke rings.

"So, Tina . . . what can I do for you?"

"Basically, I just need someone to keep writing prescriptions for my medications. With Doctor Dyer, it was never a problem. Never. In all those years. But once he left and I got stuck with Michelle, she was always making me go take blood tests for my lithium levels, and drug tests to make sure I wasn't abusing my medication, and just giving me a whole bunch of unnecessary grief for no reason whatsoever. I mean, I don't even have a car. It's hard enough to find a ride to my psychiatrist appointments—much less to all the labs and hospitals she wanted me to go to for all the stupid blood tests. Plus, she was always trying to either have me committed or to go stay in the crisis unit."

Morgan shook his head. "With your social-anxiety disorder, staying in a crisis unit with other people would be counterproductive for you."

"Exactly! That's what I always told the stupid bitch. But she wouldn't listen to me. She thought *I* was stupid. I mean, sure, I know I'm crazy. But I'm not stupid."

"Yes," Morgan said. "I can tell that already. You are definitely anything but stupid."

Tina stubbed her cigarette out, and Morgan put the ashtray back in his desk drawer.

"So tell me about yourself, Tina."

"What do you want to know?"

He looked down at the papers on his desk again. "You're twenty years old."

"Yes. Almost twenty-one."

"You look younger. I would have guessed seventeen. Do you live alone?"

"No. Never have. I live with my father and my mother."

"Here in town?"

"Yeah, over on the west side, on Circle Street."

"Did they drive you here today?"

"No. Today I had to walk."

"You walked all the way here from Circle Street?"

"Yeah. I know, right? Pretty crazy."

"Do you get along with your parents?"

"No. Never have. They are religious freaks. Total nutcases. I mean, they literally believe the planet was created two thousand years ago, and that dinosaurs are a hoax. They made me go to church three times a week when I was a kid, but I quit going when I was eleven. They couldn't make me go anymore. They tried. Oh, yes, they tried . . . but they couldn't make me. Now they hate me, and I hate them. Honestly, I wish they would just go ahead and die."

Morgan wrote some notes on a piece of paper. "What do you do for fun?"

Tina looked out the window for a moment, and then returned her gaze to the psychiatrist. "I like to sing. I love music. I took piano lessons as a child, and sang in the church choir. Then I switched to electric guitar, and started writing rock songs, but of course my parents think rock music is the devil's music, and they gave me a lot of grief about that. Mainly, these days, I just like to read."

"What do you like to read?"

"Anything I can get my hands on. I get an SSI check for my bipolar disorder. It isn't much, but almost all of it goes to e-books these days. I love to read true crime, sci-fi, horror, suspense—pretty much anything but romance."

"So, I see that your current medications are lithium for the bipolar disorder, Paxil for the manic depression, and Valium for the anxiety."

"Yes. And everything is fine, except that I need more Valium. I'm prescribed ten milligrams, but I only get sixty pills per bottle. Would you increase it to ninety per bottle, please? I really need it."

"Of course. I think it would help you."

"Thank you, Doctor Anderson. Thank you very much."

Morgan wrote three prescriptions and handed them to her.

Then he stood up. "Okay. I think we're finished here. There's a pharmacy across the street. Come on. My receptionist can lock up. I'll take you to the pharmacy, and then I'll give you a ride home. A girl as pretty as you shouldn't be walking the streets alone."

Tina smiled and stood up, too. "Thank you, Doctor Anderson. You have to be the coolest psychiatrist ever."

Chapter 4

They left before sunrise. By noon, they were halfway through Arizona. Leo drove. Jinx rode on the passenger's side.

Leo said, "I think we have a low tire."

Jinx shook his head. "Nah. It's just the fat dude in the back, making the bus lean."

"Then we'll have to get him some company, to level out the weight."

In the distance, they saw a car broken down on the side of the highway.

"And there's some more weight," Jinx said. "Straight ahead."

Leo looked in the driver's-side mirror, and saw no one behind them. No one had been behind them for miles. He slowed the bus and stopped next to the car.

A man leaned under the hood. A woman stood beside him with her arms crossed. A little girl sat in the back who appeared to be seven or eight.

Jinx put down his window. "Having a bad day, mister?"

The man closed the hood. "The fan belt broke."

Jinx got out of the bus. "It's a long walk to the nearest service station, but we're headed that way. You're more than welcome to a ride."

"Thanks. That would be great."

"Darrin," the woman said, "we don't know these people."

Darrin ran fingers through his hair. "Karen, have you seen one goddamned car since we've been stranded?"

She didn't answer.

Darrin opened the back door of the car on the driver's side. "Come on, Carrie. These people are going to take us to a service station."

Carrie got out of the car. Darrin locked its doors, and they all got in the bus. Leo started driving.

Darrin said, "We really appreciate this, guys."

"Don't mention it," Jinx said.

Moments later, Carrie said, "Mommy, why is there a fat man handcuffed to a pole back there?"

Karen said, "What are you talking about?"

"In the back, there's a fat man handcuffed to a pole."

"Stop playing around, Carrie."

"I'm not playing, Mommy. Come on, and I'll show you."

Jinx drew a pistol and pointed it at Darrin. "She's not kidding. Your bad day just got a whole lot worse."

Karen wrapped her arms around Carrie. "Please, whatever you do . . . please don't hurt my daughter."

Jinx kept his gun pointed at Darrin. "The only one who can hurt your daughter is you. If you do exactly as we say, we will not hurt your daughter."

Leo pulled over and shut the engine off.

Jinx forced Darrin, Karen, and Carrie to the back of the bus.

Leo grabbed some handcuffs from a box and followed them back. Then he pointed to the fat man. "New companions, this is Fat Bastard. Fat Bastard, meet your new companions."

Darrin said, "What the hell is going on here?"

"Stop asking questions."

"What do you want?"

"I want you to stop asking questions."

Jinx searched Darrin and Karen for weapons, found none, and confiscated their phones.

The fat man started mumbling.

Leo ungagged him. "What the fuck did I tell you?"

"I have to use the bathroom," the fat man said. "I have to go bad. I can't hold it anymore."

Leo looked at Jinx. "Give me your knife."

Jinx handed Leo a knife.

Leo grabbed the fat man by the chin and raised his face. "Open your mouth."

The fat man did not open his mouth.

Leo slashed the fat man's face. Then he pried his mouth open and cut out his tongue.

The fat man—bleeding—started screaming.

"If you don't stop screaming right this second," Leo said, "I will stab you in the goddamn eyes."

The fat man immediately stopped screaming.

Leo whistled, and Victor appeared silently from elsewhere in the bus. Leo tossed the severed tongue into the air. The Rottweiler caught it in his mouth and swallowed it.

Leo returned his gaze to the fat man. "I told you not to speak unless spoken to—and I was just about to ask you if you needed to piss. If you had waited a few more seconds, you would still have a tongue."

"Well," Carrie said, "it doesn't matter, now. He peed on himself while you were cutting him."

Leo drew a gun, pointed it at Darrin, and gave Jinx his knife back. "Take Fat Bastard to the bathroom," he told Jinx. "Let him get cleaned up."

Jinx removed the fat man's handcuffs, then forced him at gunpoint to the bathroom and waited outside the door.

After the fat man was handcuffed to the pole again, Jinx took Carrie to the bathroom. While she was away, Leo told her parents, "Look, I know Carrie is young, and she's going to talk. That's okay, as long as you keep it down. Anytime the bus stops, you don't make a peep. If you do, or if Carrie does, I'll cut all three of your tongues out. So you need to emphasize how important it is to be totally silent anytime we stop. Got it?"

They nodded.

"Excellent."

After Carrie returned, Jinx took Karen to the bathroom next, and then Darrin.

Once everyone was back, Leo handcuffed Karen's right wrist to Darrin's left wrist. Next, he handcuffed Carrie's left wrist to Darrin's right wrist. Then he cuffed the handcuffs around Darrin's left wrist to the pole.

"I'm not going to gag you," Leo said. "If you want to whisper, then go ahead and whisper. If I hear you, I'll gag you. Understand?"

Everyone nodded except the fat man, who was seated on the floor with his head down, bleeding profusely.

"Good," Leo said. "Victor will keep you company."

Chapter 5

Strickland pulled his car into a police station's parking lot. In a black suit, he got out and entered the building. He showed a receptionist his ID, which stated that he was an FBI agent. "I need to speak to Captain Harris."

"Captain Harris isn't available right now. However, you may speak to Sergeant Ridge, if you'd like."

"Is his office in the same place it was last year?"

She shrugged. "I don't know. I wasn't here last year."

"Down the hall, last door on the left?"

She nodded. "That's it."

He took off down the hall. The last door on the left was closed. Strickland didn't knock; he just walked in.

Sergeant Ridge, seated at his desk, looked up. "Hello, Agent Strickland. What brings you here?"

"I'm here to collect some evidence that we're going to use in a federal case against José Romano. We need all the coke that was seized from his home last night."

Ridge grabbed a pen, wrote something on a piece of paper, and then handed it to Strickland. "Take this to the evidence room."

Fifteen minutes later, Strickland left the station with a suitcase full of cocaine.

***

That night, Strickland parked his car in front of The Crow Bar. There were a lot of motorcycles in the parking lot. He got out holding the suitcase, approached the club's entrance, and pressed the buzzer.

A tough-looking biker opened the door. "What the fuck do you want?"

"I need to see Shark."

"Concerning?"

"Business."

"What's your name?"

"Strickland."

The biker took a phone from his pocket and pressed a button. "There's someone here named Strickland to see you." He put the phone back in his pocket. "Follow me."

The biker led him to a door in the back of the club that opened onto a staircase. They ascended the stairs and came to another door.

The biker opened the door, and they entered a room.

Shark, seated at a desk, looked up. "Agent Strickland, the only pig I know with balls enough to walk in this place. What's in the case?"

Strickland set the suitcase on the desk and opened it.

Shark looked down at the coke. "I don't need that shit."

"It's worth two million. I'll let you have it for two hundred grand."

"I'll give you fifty thousand."

"Fifty thousand?"

"Listen, pig, I've got more coke than I need—and it's undoubtedly better than this crap that you stole from the goddamn streets."

"This coke was taken during a raid on José Romano's house."

"José Romano? That piece of shit owes me money. I think I'll take this coke as partial payment."

"This isn't Romano's coke anymore," Strickland said. "It's mine, and if you want it, you'll have to buy it."

Shark drew a gun and aimed it at Strickland. "I don't have to buy a fucking thing. Now, you can either walk out of here, alive, or we can drag your dead ass out the back door. The choice is yours."

"Fine," Strickland said. "I'll take the fifty thousand."

"Fuck you, pig. That offer became nullified when I found out the product was mine. Romano owes me money, and I'm keeping the goddamn coke." Then Shark told the biker: "Get rid of this piece of shit."

"Okay, I'm leaving." Strickland turned to leave. When he got behind the biker, however, he took a gun from its holster and put it to the biker's head. "Forget about the money. I can sell the coke elsewhere. But if your friend here wants to keep his brains inside his skull, he'll grab the suitcase off your desk, and walk outside with me."

Shark told Strickland, "You're pushing your luck."

The biker grabbed Strickland's hand—the hand holding the gun—and pushed it toward the ceiling. Then he began punching him in the face while banging his hand against the wall. Eventually, Strickland dropped the gun. The biker picked it up and started bashing it against his head.

"Get him out of here," Shark said. "If you see him around here again, kill him." He then picked up a phone. "We're bringing the pig downstairs. I want his car rendered useless."

The biker kicked Strickland in the face a couple of times, then dragged him downstairs and tossed him outside.

In the parking lot, two other men shot up Strickland's car with machine guns, ruining all four tires, and all the glass.

"Give our regards to the FBI," the biker told Strickland, before slamming the pistol against his temple.

As the men went back inside, Strickland—bleeding—lost consciousness.

Chapter 6

In the back of the bus, Carrie said, "Mommy, why are those men going to kill us?"

Karen said, "We don't know for sure they're going to kill us."

"She's right, honey," Darrin said. "They might let us go if we do as they say. They told us to be quiet."

"They told us we can whisper," Karen said.

"If they're going to let us go," Carrie said, "then why did they take us?"

"I don't know," Karen said. "Maybe they're on the run from the police, and they need us as hostages."

Carrie looked over at the fat man, who was seated on the floor, still unconscious and bleeding from his mouth.

"No," she said. "I believe they're going to kill us all."

Chapter 7

Strickland woke up with a headache. He remembered everything. He reached for his gun, but it was gone. Then he reached for his phone, but it was gone, too. He knew that he must have been unconscious for a while, because the sun had not yet set when he'd arrived at The Crow Bar, and now the stars were out.

He stood up.

His car was shot to hell. The parking lot otherwise deserted. Shark and the others had apparently closed the bar and gone home.

He took off walking down the highway. He walked for maybe a mile before he saw headlights approaching. He tried to flag the car down, but it didn't stop.

He walked on.

Perhaps a mile later, he saw a bus approaching, and began waving his arms.

Chapter 8

Jinx drove.

On the passenger's side, Leo said, "Well, well, well. What do we have here?"

"Looks like roadkill to me." Jinx slowed the bus to a stop.

Leo opened his door. "What's your name, friend?"

"Strickland."

"You look like shit."

"I've had a long night," Strickland said.

"You need a ride?"

"Yes."

"Then by all means, come on in."

Strickland stepped into the bus. "Thanks so much for stopping. I really appreciate it. Can you take me to the nearest city?"

Leo closed the door. "We're taking you to Washington, D.C."

"What do you mean? I don't need to go that far."

"This bus is going to Washington, D.C., and so are you."

"What?"

Leo punched him in the face.

Strickland fell onto his back. "Who are you?"

Leo drew his pistol and aimed it at Strickland's face. "I'm someone who hates questions."

"Did Shark send you?"

"No."

"I'm a federal agent."

"I don't give a damn what you are."

"I'm serious. I was—"

Leo kicked him in the face. "I want you to shut the fuck up, and crawl to the back of the bus."

Strickland wiped blood off his face. "You don't know who you're fucking with."

Leo whistled, and Victor appeared almost instantly. He looked at the Rottweiler and said one word: "Amputate."

Victor attacked Strickland, bit down on his right wrist, and tore his hand off. Blood shot out of the stump. Strickland started screaming in agony.

Leo threw him a towel. "You might want to wrap that up."

Strickland frantically began wrapping the stump as best as he could. Leo grabbed a rope and tied the towel around the stump.

"Okay, to the back of the bus." Leo grabbed Strickland by the hair and dragged him to the back. He handcuffed a chain to the pole, then handcuffed Strickland's left wrist to the chain. "If you have to talk, you'd better whisper, or next time, Victor rips your throat out."

Leo returned to the front.

Chapter 9

In the back of the bus, Strickland looked around at his fellow captives: a man, a woman, a young girl, and a fat man who sat bleeding and unconscious. All of them, like Strickland, were either handcuffed or chained to the same pole he was.

In whispers, they exchanged names.

Darrin asked Strickland, "Where did they get you?"

"About a mile back."

"Which is where? Where are we?"

"Right outside of Oklahoma City." Strickland looked down at the bloody towel wrapped around his stump. Then he looked over at the Rottweiler, who was guarding them. "I'll probably die of an infection if I don't get to a hospital."

Darrin said, "Did they tell you anything?"

Strickland shook his head. "Only that we're going to Washington, D.C."

"Do you believe them?" Karen said.

"I don't know what to believe. How did you all get here?"

"Car broke down," Darrin said. "We were pulled off the side of the road in Arizona, and they offered us a ride to a service station."

Karen said, "I told you we should have stayed put."

"I know. God, I'm so sorry."

"Daddy," Carrie said, "don't take God's name in vain."

"I know, Carrie. I'm sorry."

Strickland looked over at the fat man, who was now awake. "What about you?"

The fat man mumbled; fresh blood flowed from his mouth.

"He was already here when they got us," Darrin said. "They had his mouth taped shut, and when he tried to ask to go to the bathroom, the white guy took a knife and cut his tongue out."

"This doesn't make any sense," Strickland said. "At first, I thought maybe they were Shark's people, but I think we can rule out that theory."

Karen said, "Who's Shark?"

Strickland shook his head. "You wouldn't know him."

Darrin said, "Do you think they'll let us go?"

Strickland held up his stump. "Look at my hand! It's gone! I don't think they're going to let anybody go."

Karen said, "Maybe they just need hostages."

Strickland sat staring at the bloody towel where his hand used to be. "Maybe they're working for the government."

"The government?" Darrin said. "What are you talking about?"

Strickland shrugged. "The government takes hostages all the time."

"For what?" Karen said.

Strickland shot her a look. "A million different reasons."

From the front came a shout: "I told you motherfuckers to whisper!"

Chapter 10

Jinx drove. "You think he's really a fed?"

On the passenger's side, Leo shrugged. "I hope so. I hate the goddamn feds." Then his phone rang, and he answered the call on speakerphone. "Hello."

"Any flies in the web?"

"Yes."

"Is the web full?"

Leo looked to the back of the bus, and smiled. "It's getting there."

"Is there anything you need?"

"No."

"Excellent. See you soon."

Leo disconnected.

Chapter 11

They heard a siren, and Jinx looked into the driver's-side mirror. "Fuck. We have company."

In his side-view mirror, Leo saw blue lights swirling behind them. "Shit. Pull over."

Jinx pulled over onto an empty stretch of the highway, and a squad car parked behind the bus.

Leo rushed to the back. "If anyone makes a peep, Victor rips your throat out." Then he returned to the front.

Two cops—a male and a female—got out and approached the bus. The male cop went to the driver's side, and the female went to Leo's.

"Driver's license," the male cop said. "Registration. Proof of insurance."

Jinx kept his hands on the steering wheel. "What the fuck you pulling me over for?"

"You have a light out."

"What light?"

"The bulb above your license plate."

"Man, you pulling me over for that weak-ass shit?"

Both cops drew their pistols. The male pointed his at Jinx; the female pointed hers at Leo.

"Juanita," the male cop said, "open the door."

Juanita opened the passenger's-side door.

"Okay, you two," the male cop said, "come out slowly with your hands up."

"All right," Jinx said. "Just take it easy, man. Chill out."

Leo stepped out first, and then Jinx followed him out on the passenger's side. When they got to the front of the bus, the male cop met them there. Both cops turned them around to face the bus. They searched them for weapons, but found none.

"You watch them," the male told Juanita, "while I search the bus."

"Wait a second," Jinx said. "Don't you need a warrant for that?"

The male looked at him. "Do you want me to get one?"

"Don't worry about it," Leo said. "We have nothing to hide. If you want to search the bus, then search the fucking bus."

The male cop stepped into the bus, leaving his partner to guard Leo and Jinx.

"Damn, baby," Jinx said, "what the fuck you doing being a cop? You should be a model, or an actress."

Juanita didn't respond, but Leo saw her crack a smile.

Then he watched the male cop walk toward the back of the bus. As he approached the back, Victor attacked him. The Rottweiler went straight for his throat. Before he ripped it open, the cop screamed.

Juanita turned her head—and Leo punched her in the temple. The blow knocked her unconscious. She started to fall, but Leo caught her. Then he grabbed her pistol and dragged her into the bus.

Chapter 12

When the dog attacked the cop, he fell backwards and landed on his back, with his feet lying near the captives. Soon thereafter, Strickland saw a small gun—a .38 revolver—tucked into a holster on the dead cop's ankle. He couldn't get the gun, because his only remaining hand was chained to the pole.

Karen was the closest one to the cop's leg.

"Get the gun!" Strickland told her.

Karen looked at it, and thought about reaching for it, but Victor growled at her before she even tried. "I can't," she said. "The dog will tear my hand off."

Chapter 13

Leo dragged Juanita—still unconscious—to the center of the bus and dropped her on the floor. Jinx came in behind them. Leo walked to the back, saw the dead cop on the floor, and heard Victor growling at Karen.

Then he saw the .38 revolver in the dead cop's ankle holster.

"Good boy, Victor." He rubbed the Rottweiler's head, looking at Karen. "You want to go for the gun?" he asked her. "Go ahead. I dare you."

Karen did nothing.

Leo took the gun from the ankle holster.

Then he dragged the cop's corpse to a large meat freezer along the driver's-side wall in the center of the bus. Excluding the pole in the back, and the bathroom, and a few shelves here and there, the meat freezer was the only thing in the bus.

Leo stuffed the corpse into the meat freezer. After he shut the lid, he handcuffed Juanita—who was still knocked out—to the meat freezer's door handle. "I hate female cops," he told Jinx, "only slightly less than I hate male cops." He then tore the uniform off her body, leaving her in only her bra and panties.

Jinx said, "What about the squad car?"

"I got it." Leo grabbed a couple of bombs from a box on one of the shelves, along with a remote-controlled detonator.

Jinx walked back up front and sat down behind the steering wheel.

Leo got out, went to the squad car behind the bus, and opened the passenger door. He placed a bomb on the dashboard, and another on the back seat. Then he closed the door and walked behind the car.

He removed the bulb above the squad car's license plate, took the good bulb with him to kneel behind the bus, and replaced the bad bulb above their license plate with the good one. Then he got back in the bus and sat down on the passenger's side.

As Jinx started the engine and drove them away, Leo pressed a button on the detonator. Behind them, the squad car exploded into flames.

Straight ahead stood a WELCOME TO ARKANSAS road sign. They crossed the Arkansas border and rode on into the night.

Chapter 14

On a street corner in Nashville, Tabitha saw another hooker she hadn't seen in a while. "Star? Oh my god! It's been forever. Where you been?"

"Hey, Tab! I've been in Denver, with Thomas. I couldn't take him anymore."

"I never liked that motherfucker."

"Me neither. I just liked his money. How you been?"

"Okay, I guess."

"Are you still with Rick?"

"No. Rick's dead."

"Dead? Damn! What happened?"

"He got in a fight with some guy in a parking lot. The dude stabbed him in the heart, and that was that."

"Oh no! That's awful. I'm so sorry."

"Yeah, Rick was a good guy."

"Did it happen here in Nashville?"

"Yeah, about a month ago. And the hard part is that we were planning to leave Nashville soon."

A car pulled up to where they stood, and the passenger's-side window came down. A man behind the steering wheel leaned over. "Are you girls on the clock?"

Star said, "Why? You on the prowl?"

He smiled. "That's one way to put it."

"What do you want?"

"How much for you and your friend?"

"You want both of us?"

"Yes."

Star looked at Tab. "What do you think?"

Tab shrugged. "Why not?"

Star told the man, "Let's go."

Tab got in the back of the car, and Star got in the front.

The man put the car in drive and headed toward an entrance ramp. Soon, they were on the interstate.

"I'm Star, and this is Tabitha."

"I'm Madison."

"Madison," Star said. "Nice name. Are you a cop?"

"No, I'm definitely not a cop."

Tab said, "Where are we going?"

He looked at her in the rearview mirror. "Where would you like to go?"

"Do you have a house?"

"Yes, I have a house."

"So let's go there."

"Can't," Madison said. "My wife and kids are there."

"Put the kids to bed," Star said, "and we'll make it a foursome."

"Nah, she would never go for that, but I know a place we can go."

Star said, "So what are you into, anyway?"

Madison handed her a piece of paper. "Look at this."

She unfolded the paper. "What is it?"

"Instructions."

"For what?"

"On how to make an incision in my scrotum with minimal bleeding."

Tab said, "What are you talking about?"

He looked at her again in the rearview mirror. "I want you to eat my testicles."

Star said, "You've got to be kidding."

"Not at all. I want each of you to eat one of my testicles."

"Star," Tab said, "I think we should get out."

"I think he's joking, Tab."

Madison shook his head. "Nope. I'm not joking."

Tab said, "Just drop us off."

Madison said nothing; he just kept driving.

Star said, "That's not really what you want, is it?"

"Yes, it is. And I'll pay you whatever you want."

Tab said, "I'm not eating your balls, mister."

"I'm with her," Star said. "Good luck finding someone to do that. You can just stop the car and let us out right here."

Madison floored the accelerator.

"What are you doing?" Star said. "Let us out!"

He laughed. "YOU WHORES ARE GOING TO EAT MY GODDAMN BALLS IF I HAVE TO FORCE-FEED THEM TO YOU!"

"Fuck you, sicko!" Star grabbed the steering wheel and yanked it to the right, making the car vibrate as it rolled over the rumble strips on the shoulder of the interstate.

Madison slammed the brakes.

Star was not wearing a seatbelt. She crashed into the windshield, bloodying her face, but suspected that her wounds were not fatal.

Madison killed the engine, and they all got out and stood on the side of the interstate.

Tab said, "What the fuck is wrong with you?"

Madison punched her in the face.

"Son of a bitch!" Star said. Then she drew a gun from her purse, shot him through the head, and he was dead before his body hit the road.

Star asked Tab, "Are you all right?"

"I'm fine. How about you?"

"I'm okay," Star said. Then she started kicking Madison's corpse. "Sick motherfucker!"

Tab said, "Want me to call the police?"

"No. Let's just try to hitch a ride to the nearest exit."

They saw headlights approaching, and began waving their arms. Moments later, a bus slowed to a stop.

A man stepped out of the bus. "What happened?"

"That guy," Tab said, pointing to Madison's corpse, "was going to kill us because we wouldn't eat his testicles."

The man looked down at the body on the ground. "Is that right?"

"Yes," Star said. "The dude was a sicko. Can you give us a ride back to the city?"

"Sure, if you put that gun away."

"Oh, I'm sorry." She put the gun back in her purse. "I'm Star, and this is Tab."

"It's a pleasure to meet you," he said. "I'm Leo."

***

Leo followed the women into the bus. "And this is Jinx," he added, before he closed the door.

Jinx moved the bus to the side of the road and killed the engine. Then he stepped out and grabbed the dead man's ankles.

Star said, "That was the craziest shit I've ever been through in my life."

"No, it wasn't." Leo pulled his gun out. "This is."

He pistol-whipped Star on the side of her head, knocking her out, and she fell unconscious to the floor. He kicked her purse aside.

Tab said, "What the fuck was that for?"

Leo aimed his gun at Tab. "No more questions." He searched her for weapons, found a phone, and put it in his pocket. Then he grabbed Star's purse off the floor.

Jinx came back inside the bus dragging the dead man's body. Leo—with his gun still aimed at Tab—opened the freezer door. Jinx dropped the dead man's body on the dead cop's corpse.

After closing the freezer door, Leo handcuffed Tab to its handle, next to the female cop. "Juanita, this is Tab. Tab, meet Juanita." Then he dragged Star—still unconscious—to the freezer, and handcuffed her to its handle, too.

Tab said, "What is going on here?"

"I'm a cop," Juanita said. "And that's my partner in the freezer."

"He's not your partner anymore," Leo said. "He's dead. And no one gave you permission to speak." He looked at Tab. "Now listen up: when your friend wakes up, you'd better tell her to be quiet, or I'll knock her right the fuck back out again. Understand?"

Tab nodded.

"Good."

Leo and Jinx returned to the front of the bus.

Jinx said, "Your turn to drive, motherfucker."

Leo sat down behind the steering wheel, started the engine, and drove them away.

On the passenger's side, Jinx lit a cigarette. "How many does that make?"

Leo thought about it. "Ten."

"That should be enough."

"Yes," Leo said. "Actually, we're a little ahead of schedule."

Taking a phone from his pocket, Jinx placed a call on speakerphone.

"Hello?"

"Cargo's almost there," Jinx said.

"Excellent. That's great to hear. Where are you?"

"We're close."

"Will you be here tomorrow?"

"Yes, we'll be there tomorrow."

"Great. I'll tell the others."

Jinx pressed END and put the phone back in his pocket.

They found a liquor store off the interstate and purchased a bottle of whiskey.

Chapter 15

They ran out of whiskey somewhere in Virginia. They needed more, but it was late and all of the liquor stores were closed.

"We could always go to a bar," Leo said.

Jinx shrugged. "Cool. Let's do it."

***

They found a club called The Ten Gallon Lounge off the interstate. They went to the back of the bus and let everyone take turns using the restroom, then handcuffed the captives back to the steel pole and the meat freezer's metal handle.

Leo whistled. Almost instantly, the massive Rottweiler joined them in the back. "We're going to go have a few drinks. If anyone makes a noise, Victor will kill you. Understand?"

Everyone nodded.

"Good."

Leo followed Jinx out of the bus and locked it.

Cars, motorcycles, and pickup trucks crowded the parking lot. Rebel flags adorned some of the trucks.

"These motherfuckers are gonna hate my black ass," Jinx said.

"Fuck these rednecks," Leo said. "They'll get over it."

They approached the entrance. Country music blasted from the interior. Jinx pressed a buzzer by the door.

A doorman opened the door. His long hair was pulled back in a ponytail. He wore a red bandanna on his head and a sleeveless leather vest over a T-shirt depicting a rebel flag. He looked at Jinx and shook his head. "No way. This is a private club, and your kind's not allowed in here, anyway."

Leo grabbed the doorman by his beard and dragged him outside. He slammed his head against the side of the cinderblock building, either killing him or knocking him unconscious. Then he dropped him on the ground in a spreading pool of blood.

They went inside. The place was packed. Illumination was bright, and cigarette smoke drifted across the air. A live band played country music to the left, and several people danced in front of the stage. Most of the men wore cowboy hats, flannel shirts, jeans, belts with large shiny buckles, and cowboy boots. Most of the women wore T-shirts, tight jeans, and cowgirl boots. Both pool tables were occupied. Four people played a game of foosball. Two men tossed darts at a dartboard. A woman rode a mechanical bull in one corner while several people whistled and cheered.

Leo followed Jinx to the bar, watching how everyone who saw Jinx gave him a funny look, but the bartender ignored them both.

Leo raised a hand and signaled the bartender over. The man approached them, but didn't speak. Leo said, "Do I have to come across this bar and get a drink myself?"

The bartender—like most of the other men in the establishment—wore a cowboy hat. He crossed his arms. "I wouldn't suggest it."

"Then you need to hop on your pony and bring us a bottle of whiskey."

The bartender uncrossed his arms and put his hands on his hips. "What did you say?"

Like Jinx, Leo had elected not to sit down on a stool. Still standing, he leaned closer over the bar. "I said that you need to hop on your pony, *cowboy,* and bring my friend and me a bottle of whiskey."

"We don't sell whiskey by the bottle."

Leo pulled his gun out. He placed it on the bar with his finger on the trigger and the muzzle pointed at the bartender. "You can either bring us a bottle of whiskey, or we'll kill you and everyone in here."

The bartender looked at the gun, and then he looked at Leo. "Fine. Fifty bucks."

Jinx handed the man a hundred-dollar bill. "Keep the change."

The bartender put the money in his pocket instead of the cash register. Then he gave Jinx a bottle of whiskey.

Leo put his gun away.

Jinx broke the seal on the bottle. He took a drink and handed it to Leo. Then they started walking around the club, passing the whiskey back and forth.

The band finished the song they were playing. The singer said, "We'll be back in a few!"

Jinx said, "Where exactly are we, anyway?"

"Virginia."

"I know we're in Virginia, motherfucker. I mean, what's the name of this goddamn town?"

"I don't know," Leo said. "I don't remember."

Jinx took a drink. "I don't like this fucking town."

A cowboy approached them, obviously drunk. "I think you boys are in the wrong fucking bar." He pointed at Jinx. "Especially you."

Jinx gave the bottle to Leo. Then he grabbed the man's wrist with one hand, his index finger with the other, and snapped it. The man shrieked. Leo pulled his gun out and pistol-whipped the man, knocking him out. Jinx released the man's wrist and he fell to the floor, unconscious.

Everyone in the vicinity had noticed the altercation, and a few cowboys surrounded them.

A large man—presumably a bouncer—approached them. "I think it's time for you fellas to leave."

"That's funny," Leo said. "I was thinking the same thing." Then he kicked the bouncer in the knee, hard enough that he heard something snap. The bouncer leaned forward, his face contorted with pain, and Jinx karate-chopped him in the throat. The bouncer started gagging, holding his throat, and swayed on his feet. Then Leo kicked him in the other knee, and the bouncer fell.

More cowboys surrounded them. Leo swung his pistol in their direction, and Jinx pulled an Uzi from beneath his trench coat.

One of the cowboys said, "What are you gonna do, shoot us all?"

"I suppose we're going to have to," Leo said. "Starting with you." He shot him between the eyes, and then Jinx sprayed the rest of them with the Uzi. Perhaps ten cowboys fell over, dead.

"Does anyone else have anything to say?" Leo said.

No one in the club said a word.

Leo took a drink, and then gave the bottle to Jinx. Jinx took a drink and set the bottle on a table.

Leo said, "I suppose we'd better leave."

Jinx nodded. "Cool."

They left.

Outside, as they walked toward the bus, two men— one fat; one thin—wearing cowboy hats crossed their path in the parking lot.

The skinny one looked at Jinx. Then he told his friend, "Damn, Earl, I didn't know they let *coons* in this place."

Jinx sprayed him with the Uzi, and he was dead before he hit the pavement.

Earl looked down at his dead companion. When he looked back up, Leo clubbed him alongside the head with his pistol, knocking him out. Earl hit the ground twitching, and then was still.

"This town is like a goddamn twilight zone," Jinx said.

"No shit. Help me drag his fat ass to the bus."

They got him in the bus and dragged him to the back, where Victor was watching over the hostages. They handcuffed Earl to the pole, and none of the other captives said a word.

They returned to the front of the bus. Leo sat down behind the steering wheel, and Jinx sat down on the passenger's side.

"Shit," Jinx said. "I left the whiskey in the club."

"No big deal. Let's go get it. But since we just got Earl, let's get rid of that corpse we picked up in Nashville."

They removed the corpse from atop the dead cop in the freezer and carried it out of the bus. They dropped it on the parking lot, and then Leo locked the bus.

They approached the club. The door was locked. Leo retrieved his pistol, shot the lock a couple of times, and kicked the door open.

They entered the club. Everyone stayed out of their way as they walked over the dead bodies to the table upon which Jinx had left their whiskey. Jinx grabbed the bottle, and they turned to leave.

Then about ten cops entered the club with their guns drawn.

A woman pointed at Leo and Jinx. "That's them!"

The cops aimed their guns at Leo and Jinx. One of the cops said, "Hands in the air!"

Jinx took a drink of whiskey. Then he gave the bottle to Leo. Leo took a drink and set the bottle on the table.

Another cop said, "Hands in the goddamn air!"

Leo and Jinx raised their hands.

The cops approached them.

Leo said, "You'd better shoot us."

The cops attacked them and slammed them to the floor. They searched them and took Leo's pistol and Jinx's Uzi, along with several knives, spare clips, and a couple of hand grenades.

"You have the right to remain silent," a cop said.

Leo said, "You should have shot us."

"Anything you say can and will be used against you in a court of law."

Leo smiled. "You're going to die tomorrow night."

"You have the right to an attorney."

"If you're married, I'm going to kill your wife."

"If you can't afford an attorney, one will be appointed to you."

"I'm going to kill her because she married a goddamn pig."

The cops took them out in handcuffs. There were a lot of squad cars in the parking lot, but—to Leo's surprise—the cops put him and Jinx in the same car.

The arresting officer drove them away. Leo stared at their bus in the parking lot until it vanished in the distance.

"After I kill your wife," Leo said, "I'm going to feed her to my dog."

The cop looked at him in the rearview mirror. "If the two of you *don't* get the death penalty, you'll most definitely both die in prison."

Jinx said, "We're not going to prison, and by this time tomorrow night, your ass will be as dead as all those cowboys back there in the club."

"Whatever." The cop turned on the radio. A country-music song began to play.

Chapter 16

The squad car pulled into a police station's parking lot. Two more squad cars parked behind it. The arresting officer got out, and two more cops met him at his car. They opened both of the squad car's rear doors.

The arresting officer grabbed Leo by his arm and pulled him out of the car.

"Take your fucking hands off me, pig," Leo said.

The cop did not respond. Nor did he remove his hands from Leo's arm.

"I won't be in handcuffs tomorrow night," Leo said. "Tomorrow night, my hands will be free."

Another cop pulled Jinx out of the car.

"I wanna make a phone call," Jinx said.

"You'll make a phone call," the cop said, "when we tell you that you can."

Jinx asked Leo, "How many pigs can we fit in the freezer?"

"We can fit these two," Leo said, "definitely."

Once in the station, the cops took them into a room with a table, some chairs, and nothing else.

"Y'all gonna be some dead fucking pigs," Jinx said, "very soon."

"I'll bring you a phone," the arresting officer said.

He left the room.

Chapter 17

The arresting officer stepped into an office.

Another cop sat behind a desk. "How bad was it?"

"Fourteen dead. Twelve in the club, and two in the parking lot. They could have gotten away, but they went back inside because they forgot a bottle of liquor."

"They don't sound very bright."

"They're not. I'm gonna let them make a call, and then I'll see if I can get them to sign a confession."

From a filing cabinet, he retrieved an old landline telephone and took it with him when he left.

Chapter 18

The arresting officer came back with a telephone. He plugged its cord into a jack and set the phone on the table. "Make your call."

Jinx picked up the receiver and made a call. Moments later, he spoke into the phone: "The robot needs repaired." Then he looked up at the cop. "Where are we?"

"Hillsville, Virginia."

"We're in Hillsville, Virginia." Jinx hung up the phone.

"I can't wait until tomorrow," Leo told the cop. "Victor's gonna love you."

"Victor?" the cop said. "Is that your dog?"

"If you have a wife, I advise you to send her away for twenty-four hours."

The cop scratched his head. "Are you retarded?"

"Sometimes."

"If you don't get the death penalty, you're going to die in prison."

"No, I'm not. And you're gonna die within twenty-four hours."

"What are you going to do? Have one of your friends come after me?"

"No," Leo said. "I'm killing you myself."

"You don't scare me."

"I know. You're too stupid to be scared."

"Whatever." The cop left the room and closed the door.

Chapter 19

Earl woke up handcuffed to the pole in the back of the bus. With a killer headache, he looked around at the other captives and the massive Rottweiler. "What's going on here?"

Strickland held up the stump where his hand used to be. The bloody towel wrapped around it was still dripping. "You'd better do as they say."

"Where are we?"

"You tell us," Darrin said. "We haven't moved since they brought you on the bus."

"We're in Hillsville," Earl said. "Hillsville, Virginia."

Strickland said, "They're taking us to Washington, D.C."

"D.C.? Why are they taking us to D.C.?"

"I don't know," Strickland said. "I've been asking myself that question since they picked me up in Oklahoma City."

Carrie said, "They're taking us there to kill us."

Karen put her free arm around her daughter. "We don't know that, honey. They might let us go."

"No," Carrie said. "They're going to kill us all. They're not letting anybody go."

Chapter 20

In Hillsville, Virginia, Federal Agent Ludwig pulled his car into the police station's parking lot. He got out, entered the building, and encountered a police officer in a hallway. "I need to speak to your supervisor immediately."

"Who are you?"

He flashed an ID card, which stated that he worked for the FBI. "Federal Agent Ludwig."

The cop nodded. "Follow me." He led Ludwig down the hallway to an open door, and Ludwig followed the cop into the room. A man dressed in plain clothes looked up from some paperwork on his desk.

"Captain," the cop said, "this is Agent Ludwig with the FBI."

The captain stood up and extended a hand. "I'm Captain Jarrell."

Ludwig shook his hand. "I need you to take me to the murder suspects."

"Mind if I ask why?"

"If they're who we think they are, they'll have to come with me."

"I see," Jarrell said. "Okay. I'll take you to them."

Jarrell and the cop led Ludwig to the one-way window that looked into the interrogation room. They saw Leo and Jinx handcuffed and shackled to separate chairs.

"That's them," Ludwig said. "Captain Jarrell, these suspects are now in the custody of the Federal Bureau of Investigation." He withdrew a document from his jacket and handed it to Jarrell.

Jarrell looked at the piece of paper. "I'll have to make a couple of phone calls."

Ludwig nodded. "Of course."

Jarrell walked away.

Ludwig, while staring at Leo and Jinx through the one-way window, told the cop, "These two have been on our most-wanted list for a long time. We'll be glad to finally have them in custody."

Jarrell returned moments later. "Everything checks out. They're all yours."

Ludwig said, "I was told that you found some weapons in their possession. I'm going to need those, too."

The cop nodded. "Be right back." He went to the evidence room, and then returned with a duffel bag containing the weapons. "Here you go." He handed the bag to Ludwig.

They entered the interrogation room. Ludwig withdrew two sets of handcuffs from his jacket. "Uncuff them."

The cop removed their handcuffs and shackles, then Ludwig handcuffed their wrists with his own.

Jarrell and the cop escorted them out of the building. Ludwig put Leo and Jinx in the back of his car.

Ludwig shook hands with Jarrell and the cop. "Gentlemen," he said, "thanks for your cooperation." Then he got in his car and drove away.

Ludwig looked at Leo and Jinx in the rearview mirror. "I had the crime scene evacuated, and I'm taking you back to the bus. We expect you in D.C. tomorrow."

They rode in silence.

***

Ludwig pulled his car into the empty parking lot at The Ten Gallon Lounge. He parked beside the bus, killed the engine, then got out and opened the rear door on the driver's side.

Leo and Jinx got out of the car. Ludwig removed their handcuffs.

Then he handed Jinx the duffel bag. "Here are your things. See you tomorrow."

He got back in his car and drove away.

Chapter 21

Leo drove the bus.

Jinx rode next to him on the passenger's side. "Got any more of that coke?"

"I thought you hated cocaine."

"Shit, after the night we've had, I'm ready to get high on goddamn *something.*"

"Sorry about your luck," Leo said, "but I'm all out."

"That figures."

The radio was already at low volume, but Leo turned it all the way down. "We could go see the doctor, though, if you want to."

"The doctor?"

"Yeah, man. We're actually not too far from his house. I mean, we don't have to be in D.C. for several hours, and we're already almost there. We may was well stock up on cocaine."

Jinx nodded. "Cool. Let's go see the doctor."

Chapter 22

Doctor Morgan Anderson sat on a rocking chair in his living room, dressed in a robe and wearing spectacles, reading a thick hardback book to the muffled sounds of a gagged woman screaming downstairs in the basement.

His doorbell rang.

Morgan closed the book. According to the digital clock on the mantel above the fireplace, the time was 4:06 a.m. He set the book down on the floor, retrieved his pistol from beneath the rocking chair, then got up and went to the door.

Through the one-way peephole, he saw Leo and Jinx standing on the front porch. Smiling, Morgan shook his head.

Then he unlocked the door.

Chapter 23

Leo drew his gun. Then he pressed the doorbell. Beside him, Jinx had his pistol up and ready.

Seconds later, Doctor Morgan Anderson opened the door. "Hello, Leo. Hello, Jinx. Long time no see. What brings you to the east coast?"

"Long story," Leo said, looking down at Morgan's pistol, which was pointed at the living-room floor. Both he and Jinx had their guns aimed at the doctor. "But we need some cocaine."

Morgan nodded. "Well, you've certainly come to the right place. Perhaps if you'd lower those guns, I'd invite you in."

Leo and Jinx lowered their pistols.

Morgan stepped to the left. "Come on in."

They entered the living room. Morgan closed the door and locked it.

Less than a second later, after a woman somewhere beneath them started screaming, Leo and Jinx aimed their guns at the doctor.

"Who the fuck is that screaming?" Leo said.

Morgan's gun was still pointed at the floor. "A patient of mine."

"Patient?"

"Well . . . *prisoner,* now. Tina Miller. Twenty years old. Bipolar-one disorder. Social anxiety. Borderline schizophrenia. Trailer trash, basically. But drop-dead gorgeous. No siblings. She lived with her parents until I killed them, and then I brought her here."

Jinx shook his head. "You are one sick motherfucker."

Morgan laughed. "Coming from someone in your line of work, I'll take that as a compliment." He set his pistol on the coffee table. "Are you gentlemen going to keep pointing those guns at me all night, or do you want me to go get you some cocaine?"

Leo shoved his gun into the waistband of his jeans, and Jinx returned his pistol to the holster beneath his trench coat.

Morgan opened a liquor cabinet. "Care for something to drink?"

"Whiskey," Leo said. "No ice."

Jinx said, "Same for me."

Morgan filled two glasses with whiskey, and handed one to each.

Jinx took a drink. "Good stuff. Thank you very much."

"You're welcome. Now, how much cocaine do you want?"

Leo took a drink. "We want it all."

"All of it?"

Jinx said, "Everything you have."

"I have quite a bit. You're talking about a whole lot of money."

Jinx pulled a large wad of hundred-dollar bills from his pocket. "There's plenty more out in the bus."

Morgan nodded. "Very well. I shall return." He left the room.

Beneath them, the screaming began again—no words, just muffled roars and shouts. To Leo, the screaming sounded more like expressions of anger than of pain.

Jinx sipped his whiskey. "Damn, somebody is *pissed.*"

Leo nodded. "Yeah. I'd be pissed off, too, if some psycho had me locked up in his basement."

Morgan came back into the room moments later. He set a briefcase on the coffee table and opened it. Inside the briefcase were numerous bags of white powder. "Premium cocaine, my friends. The highest quality. Better go get some more money out of your bus."

Jinx withdrew his silencer-fitted pistol and raised it. "We're not your friends." Then he shot the doctor between the eyes, killing him instantly.

Beneath them, the screaming began again.

Leo said, "What did he say her name was?"

Jinx returned his pistol to its holster. "Tina Miller."

"That's it. Tina Miller. Should we add her to the collection?"

Jinx shook his head. "Nah, man. There's no need. We have enough already."

Each took another drink of whiskey.

"Should we go check her out?" Leo said. "See what kind of condition she's in?"

"Couldn't hurt. I mean, if she's real bad off, I suppose we could put her out of her misery."

"Yeah, that would be fucked up to just leave her down there."

Jinx shrugged. "Then let's go check her out."

They finished their whiskeys and set the empty glasses on the coffee table, next to the briefcase. Then they found a door to the basement and went downstairs.

The basement's concrete floor was wet. The cinderblock walls were slimy with black mold. Leo saw countless spiders living in numerous webs, but the number of dead white spiders dangling from the ceiling was even higher. A sump pump sucked water down a hole in the center of the floor.

Tina Miller was confined to a corner of the basement. Her mouth was gagged with cloth, and her wrists were bound by rope tied to an ancient-looking radiator. She saw them immediately, and began screaming through the cloth and tugging violently at her rope. She was skinny, dressed only in a T-shirt and panties. Her hair and flesh were as filthy as her clothes.

Leo found her attractive nevertheless. When Jinx shot him a look, Leo could tell by his eyes that Jinx found her attractive, also.

They approached her. She continued making a lot of noise and thrashing against her rope.

From his back pocket, Jinx produced a switchblade knife and opened it. "Hold still, and I'll cut you loose."

She immediately became silent and motionless, and then Jinx cut her loose.

She removed the gag herself. "Thank you. Where is that son of a bitch?"

"Dead," Jinx said. "We killed him."

Tina cocked her head. "Who the fuck are you two? Never mind. I'm so hungry, I don't even care." She dashed past them and raced up the stairs.

Leo and Jinx looked at each other. Leo cracked a smile, and Jinx shook his head. Then both headed up the stairs.

They found Tina in the kitchen, standing in front of the open refrigerator, shoving slices of bologna into her mouth with one hand, while holding a gallon of milk with the other. She turned around and glared at them as she ate.

Leo looked at Jinx, trying not to laugh, and Jinx returned his stare with another shake of his head. Both shrugged, and then returned to the living room.

They stepped around Morgan's corpse on their way to the sofa.

Jinx sat down, retrieved a bag from the briefcase, and stabbed it with his switchblade knife. Then he licked the blade. "Damn. The doctor wasn't lying. This is some premium cocaine."

"You want some more whiskey?"

"Of course."

Leo took their glasses to the liquor cabinet. Jinx chopped out lines on the coffee table. Moments later, both sniffed cocaine on the sofa with a hundred-dollar bill rolled cylindrically. Then they each took sips of whiskey and fired up a cigarette.

Tina joined them soon thereafter in the living room. She held a package of bologna, a package of cheese, a loaf of bread, and the gallon of milk. She sat down on the rocking chair, took a few gulps of milk, and set the jug down on the floor. Then she unwrapped a few slices of cheese, made a big bologna sandwich, and proceeded to eat.

Leo and Jinx watched her, and Tina stared right back. Her eyes darted back and forth between them. Leo thought she didn't look afraid of them at all. He thought she still looked angry, or maybe she was just deranged.

"Damn, girl," Jinx said. "You ain't gonna put no mayonnaise on that, or nothing?"

Chewing, Tina shook her head, glaring at him. Then she swallowed. "I fucking hate mayonnaise."

"What about mustard? You like mustard?"

Tina shook her head, and then took another bite.

"Damn," Jinx said. "I couldn't be eating no fucking dry bologna sandwich."

Tina swallowed, and then took a drink of milk. "Do I look like I give a fuck what you could or couldn't eat?" She set the jug back down on the floor, and resumed eating.

Leo finished his cigarette and took a sip of whiskey.

Jinx—on the end of the sofa nearest Tina's rocking chair—finished his cigarette, and snorted another line. Then he offered Tina the rolled-up, hundred-dollar bill. "Want some coke? It's top-grade shit."

Chewing, Tina shook her head again. Then she swallowed. "Hell, no. Are you kidding me? My head would spin right the fuck off my shoulders. I did cocaine once, and hated it. Talk about bouncing off the goddamn walls. Never again." She resumed eating.

Leo sipped his whiskey, and lit another cigarette.

Jinx drew his pistol, aimed it at Tina's face—and she didn't blink. She just kept eating.

"Damn, girl," Jinx said. "I could have just blown your brains all over the wall behind you, and you didn't even flinch. You are one stone-cold motherfucker. I like that."

Tina did not respond. She just kept eating and staring into his eyes, not even looking at the gun.

Jinx lowered the pistol and held it by his leg. "Before I put a bullet through his head, Doctor Anderson told us you were bipolar and borderline schizophrenic."

Tina finished her sandwich, and then gulped from the gallon of milk. "The son of a bitch killed my parents. Happiest night of my fucking life. Told me he was there to rescue me. Then he brought me here and tied me up in the basement. I don't even know how long I've been here. He didn't give me my meds, almost never fed me, and rarely even brought me any water. He did other things, though. A goddamn sicko. I'm sure you can imagine."

"That's fucked up," Jinx said. "For real. I'm sorry you had to go through some shit like that."

Tina asked Leo, "May I have one of those cigarettes, please?"

He got up, brought her a cigarette, and lit it for her.

"Thank you."

"Don't mention it." He returned to the sofa.

Jinx asked Tina, "So what do you want us to do with you?"

She cocked her head. "What do you mean?"

"Well, I mean, I guess we're not going to kill you. So do you want us to just let you walk out of here? Do you want us to drop you off somewhere? Do you want to just stay here, when we leave? It's totally up to you."

"I have nowhere to go, except back to my dead parents' trailer, and I'd honestly rather go anywhere but there." She flipped ashes onto the floor. "Just take me with you, wherever you're going, until I figure out what to do."

Jinx looked over at Leo, and chuckled.

"What the fuck's so funny?" Tina said. "I get SSI every month. And food stamps. And Medicaid. I'll be okay. I just need to figure out what the fuck I'm gonna do."

Jinx sipped his whiskey. "I don't even think we've introduced ourselves yet. I'm Jinx, this is my friend Leo, and you are sitting in a dead psychiatrist's living room with two of the most dangerous motherfuckers on planet Earth."

"I need some Valium," Tina said. "And not because you're so goddamn *dangerous,* or whatever. I haven't been taking my meds, and my nerves are shot." She looked down at Morgan's corpse. "I know this piece of shit has some Valium around here somewhere. You mind if I look around?"

Jinx shook his head. "Knock yourself out."

Tina left the room. Leo and Jinx sipped whiskey while listening to the sounds of her searching a nearby room.

She returned moments later, rattling a bottle of pills. "Found them. Medicine cabinet in the bathroom. Valium Tens." She removed the lid, poured several pills into her mouth from the bottle, and washed them down with milk. "I'll be better soon."

She looked at their lowball glasses on the coffee table. "What are you guys drinking?" Then she saw the liquor cabinet. "Never mind."

She went to the liquor cabinet, grabbed a fifth of vodka, and began taking shots from the bottle while pacing around the room.

Leo looked over at Jinx—who seemed as impressed by Tina's drinking as he was—and then resumed watching Tina's lunacy.

"Hot damn!" she said. "I feel better already! I'll feel *much* better after these Valiums kick in. So, can I go with you guys, or not?"

Jinx asked Leo, "What do you think?"

Leo shrugged. "I don't see why not." Then he told Tina, "But we *do* have a busload of hostages parked out front. Would you have a problem with that?"

"Not at all. And you don't have to explain. I don't even want to know. But how big of a hurry are you in to leave?"

Leo looked at the clock on the mantel above the fireplace. "Not a *big* hurry. Why?"

She stopped pacing and took a shot of vodka. "Because I'm filthy, and would like to take a shower. I'll be fast. Do we have time?"

Leo nodded. "Sure. Go take a shower."

Tina set the bottle on the coffee table. "Back in a flash."

***

In the bathroom, Tina removed her T-shirt and panties, and added them to the trash. Then she showered as fast as she could, running the water so hot she could barely stand it, washing her hair and the rest of her body with a dead man's shampoo. Afterward, she squirted toothpaste on a finger and brushed her teeth.

In Morgan's bedroom, she searched his clothes for something to wear. She settled on black boxers, black socks, black sweatpants, and a black T-shirt.

She went back into the living room with wet hair. "Fast enough?"

Leo and Jinx still sat on the sofa.

"Yes," Leo said. "And you clean up nicely, by the way."

Jinx sipped his whiskey. "Yes. Nicely, indeed."

Tina smiled. "Those Valiums are kicking in. Or maybe the vodka. Or maybe it's just that shower-fresh feeling. Whatever it is, I feel great. So, where are we going, anyway?"

Leo said, "Washington, D.C."

Tina grabbed the bottle of vodka and took a drink. "Seriously? That's awesome! I've never been there! Which is sad, I know, considering how close it is to where I live. Or *used* to live, anyway. My parents never goddamn took me anywhere."

Leo and Jinx finished their whiskeys and rose from the sofa.

"We have a guard dog on the bus," Leo said. "A Rottweiler named Victor. We'll introduce you to him. After that, stay up front near us, away from all the hostages. Think you can manage that?"

Tina smiled. "Right now, I feel like I can manage anything."

Jinx grabbed two bottles of whiskey from the liquor cabinet. Leo grabbed the briefcase full of cocaine. Tina, still holding her bottle of vodka, grabbed another bottle for the road.

The three of them left the house and went outside into the still-dark morning. There was no traffic in the neighborhood at that hour, and the sodium-vapor lamps along the street were still aglow.

"That's a big fucking bus," Tina said, as they approached it.

Jinx opened the door on the passenger's side, got in and stepped across, then sat down behind the steering wheel. Tina followed him inside. Leo, carrying the briefcase, got in last and closed the door.

Leo whistled, and Tina watched the biggest Rottweiler she had ever seen approach them from the back. Leo grabbed her hand and held it up to the Rottweiler's nose. "Victor, this is Tina. She's a friend."

Victor licked her hand and wagged his tail.

Tina looked beyond the dog, into the back of the bus. Illumination was minimal, but she saw several hostages nevertheless.

Jinx fired up the bus. "Better find yourself a seat, Tina. We're leaving."

She turned to Leo. "Mind if I sit on your lap?"

He put the briefcase behind the passenger's seat. "Not at all." He sat down.

Tina sat down on his lap. Straight ahead, to the east, the sky was turning gold and pink with the first light of morning.

Jinx turned on the radio, and then they hit the road.

Chapter 24

Tina woke up on Leo's lap. Still holding the bottle of vodka, she took a drink. Beyond the windshield, she saw a few historic landmarks of Washington, D.C. that she recognized from TV and magazines. "We're here already?"

"Yes," Leo said.

"How long have I been asleep?"

"Not long. Only about an hour, or so."

Soon thereafter, Jinx drove them to what Tina thought had to be an abandoned warehouse. He parked the bus in front of the building, which was massive. There were no other vehicles in the parking lot.

Jinx killed the engine. "We're early, so we'll have to sit out here and chill for a little bit." Then he told Leo, "Let me hit that whiskey."

Leo handed him the bottle. Jinx took a drink and gave the bottle back.

Tina took a drink of vodka, staring at the building through the windshield. "Is that a warehouse?"

"I think it used to be," Leo said, "a long time ago. And I guess it's still a warehouse, in a way."

"But now it's empty?"

"No," Jinx said. "This place is never empty. The powers that be just want it to look that way from the street."

"So you've been here before?"

"Yes, many times. Leo and I have been coming here for years. It's what we do."

"What do you mean?"

"It's our job," Leo said. "Driving from L.A. to D.C. once a month is what Jinx and I do for a living."

Tina turned around and looked at the hostages in the back, then looked out the windshield at the warehouse again. She took a drink of vodka. "So where are you two going after this?"

"Back to Virginia," Leo said. "To kill a cop."

"That sounds fun! Can I go with you?"

Leo and Jinx exchanged glances. Jinx shrugged.

"Sure," Leo said. "I don't see why not."

"Awesome! And I want to thank you guys again for rescuing me. Seriously. I appreciate it."

Leo took a drink. "Don't mention it."

Tina lit a cigarette. "So where are you going after you kill the cop?"

"After that," Jinx said, "we're going home."

"Where do you live?"

"California."

"Can I come with you? Just until I figure out what I'm gonna do? I've never been anywhere, really, and I've always wanted to go to California."

Leo and Jinx exchanged glances again, and shrugged.

"Sure," Leo said. "You can stay with us for a while."

"Thanks! Do you two live together?"

Leo nodded. "We share a compound in Los Angeles."

"Awesome! You guys may not be able to get rid of me."

Jinx checked his wristwatch. "We should let the hostages use the restroom." From beneath the driver's seat, he retrieved a silencer-fitted pistol and handed it to Tina. "You know how to use one of these?"

"Of course," she said. "Just aim and pull the trigger."

"That's right. Just aim and pull the trigger. The safety's off, and there's a bullet in the chamber. You can take the girls to the restroom, and Leo can take the guys. I'll stay up here and guard the front."

Tina nodded. "I can do that."

Thirty minutes later, after meeting and learning the names of all the hostages in the bus, she followed Leo back to the front.

"It's about that time," Jinx told her. "We're going in the warehouse now, and you're coming with us. If we end up having to shoot motherfuckers, we'll expect you to start shooting people, too. Understand?"

"Absolutely."

They all three got out on the passenger's side, and then Jinx pressed a button on his key fob, locking the bus.

Tina shoved the pistol into the waistband at the front of her sweatpants, but had to keep a grip on the handle to keep it from falling. She swept her gaze across the parking lot. Excluding their bus, the parking lot was empty. She followed Leo and Jinx to a door on the side of the building.

Leo pressed a buzzer by a keypad.

Moments later, a man in a black tuxedo opened the door. "Hello, Leo. Hello, Jinx. It's good to see you again." Then he looked at Tina. "Who's your friend?"

"Hello, Bennett," Leo said. "This is Tina."

He nodded. "It's a pleasure to meet you, Tina."

"Likewise."

Bennett backed up and stepped to the side. "Come on in."

Leo went in first. Jinx followed him in.

Then Tina stepped into a ballroom. The ceiling was high. Crystal chandeliers provided bright illumination. Classical music played at low volume. Mirrors on the walls produced an illusion that the ballroom was even larger than it was. The color scheme was red: the walls were red; the ceiling was red; the scarlet floor was so polished it resembled a frozen lake of blood. There were red floral arrangements everywhere. Red tablecloths covered red banquet tables. Red napkins were folded on red tablecloths. Crimson carpet covered spiral staircases that ascended to upper levels.

The ballroom—abuzz with conversation—was packed with men in white tuxedos and women in white dresses and ball gowns. A roaming wait staff served champagne and cocktails throughout.

"Follow me," Bennett said. "I'll take you to Senator Fox."

He led them across the ballroom. Tina noticed that all the dinner plates on the banquet tables were empty.

They followed him through a door into a shipping-and-receiving area with a concrete floor and cinderblock walls. Two men stood near a row of garage doors, and they approached them. One of the men wore a black suit. The other man wore a black tuxedo.

Leo told Bennett, "We can handle it from here."

"Very well." Bennett turned and headed back to the ballroom.

The man in the black suit smiled. "Hello, Leo. Hello, Jinx." Then he looked at Tina. "Who's your friend?"

"Hello, Senator Fox," Leo said. "This is Tina."

He nodded at Tina. "Nice to meet you." Then he asked Leo and Jinx, "How have you been?"

"Peachy," Jinx said. "How are you?"

Fox rubbed his stomach. "We're hungry." Then he and the other man started laughing.

Tina noticed that Leo and Jinx didn't laugh.

The senator stopped laughing. "I heard you killed some rednecks in Virginia."

Leo lit a cigarette. "Shit happens."

Fox nodded. "Where's the meat wagon?"

"Parked around front," Jinx said. "You want us to bring it in?"

"Yes. You know the routine. Just pull it around back and bring it in through there." Fox pointed at the garage doors. "We'll have one of those open when you get here."

Tina followed Leo and Jinx back to the ballroom. They crossed it and went outside. Jinx unlocked the bus and they all got in.

"I can't stand that motherfucker," Jinx said.

"I know what you mean," Leo said. "I hate politicians. Want me to drive?"

Jinx gave him the keys, and Leo drove the bus around the building, to the back of the warehouse. One of the garage doors was open, and he drove through. Senator Fox stood smiling in the shipping-and-receiving area, waving them in, and Tina saw that the man beside him now held a shotgun.

Leo killed the engine. Then Tina followed him and Jinx to the freezer in the middle of the bus—where Juanita, Tab, and Star stood handcuffed to the freezer's handle.

Leo removed Tab's handcuffs and shoved her toward Jinx, who grabbed her by an arm and put a gun to her head. Then Leo removed Star's handcuffs.

"Where are you taking us?" Star said.

Leo backhanded her across the face, busting her nose and lips. "If I hear another word out of you, I'm gonna tell Victor to eat you."

Tina watched the Rottweiler lick his lips. She also saw that his tail wasn't wagging.

Then she followed Leo and Jinx as they dragged the two women out of the bus, where Senator Fox and the man with the shotgun stood waiting. Another man joined them, then he and the man with the shotgun grabbed the women and dragged them away.

Fox smiled. "Great work, gentlemen. They look tasty."

"Spare us the bullshit," Jinx said. "Just pay us our money, and we'll bring the rest of them in. Then we'll be on our way."

"Leaving so soon, gentlemen? We'd be delighted to treat you to dinner. Why not join us in the feast?"

"Can't," Leo said. "We have to go back to Hillsville to kill some cops."

Fox picked up a briefcase and handed it to Jinx. "Here's your money. Your services, as always, are appreciated."

More words were exchanged, but Tina wasn't listening. Instead, she watched the two men drag Star and Tab through a set of open doors behind the senator into a hallway lined with freezer doors. From where she stood, each freezer appeared to be the size of a prison cell. The man dragging Star by the hair withdrew a pistol and shot her once through the head, killing her instantly. When Tab started screaming, the man with the shotgun blew her head off. Then the two men put the corpses in separate freezers and closed the doors.

"Come on," Leo told her. "Time to unload some more cargo."

She followed him and Jinx back inside the bus.

***

In the back, the fat man with no tongue—now wide awake—made unintelligible noise, and blood continued flowing from his mouth.

On the floor, Carrie looked up at her father. "Are you still a Christian, Daddy?"

Karen said, "Of course he's still a Christian."

"I'm not talking to you, Mommy. I know you're still a Christian." Carrie looked back up at her father. "But Daddy, you say a lot of bad words, and you never go to church anymore."

Darrin forced a smile. "Carrie, honey, now is not the time."

"But they're going to kill us, Daddy. And if you're not a Christian, you won't go to Heaven with me and Mommy."

Leo interrupted their conversation. "Sermon's over, people."

Tina stood next to Jinx, who aimed an Uzi at the captives. Victor stood next to Tina.

Leo removed Darrin's handcuffs first, and then Strickland's. The gory towel wrapped around Strickland's stump at the end of his arm was dripping blood.

Strickland said, "I need to get to a hospital."

Tina followed Leo and Jinx as they forced the two men out of the bus. Then she watched the two gunmen force them into the hallway of freezers.

The man with the pistol shot Darrin through the head, killing him instantly.

The other man aimed his shotgun at Strickland.

"Wait, please!" Strickland said. "I'm a federal agent, and I need to get to a hospital!"

The man blew Strickland's head off. Then the gunmen put both corpses in a freezer and closed the door.

Senator Fox followed Leo, Jinx, and Tina into the bus, stopping in the middle when he saw a woman in a bra and panties handcuffed to a meat freezer's handle. He stroked her hair. "Well, well, well. What's your name, honey?"

She didn't answer.

"This bitch is a cop," Jinx told him. "Her name's Juanita."

Leo removed her handcuffs and shoved her toward the senator. She struggled, but Fox backhanded her, and she stopped resisting. Then Leo and Jinx lifted her dead partner out of the freezer, and Tina followed them all out of the bus.

While Fox dragged Juanita into the hallway, Leo and Jinx carried her dead partner. After the man with the shotgun nodded at an empty freezer, Leo and Jinx tossed the corpse inside. The man with the handgun closed the door.

With a fistful of Juanita's hair, Senator Fox told her, "I'm anxious to taste your flesh after it's cooked."

She looked into his eyes. "You're sick."

"So are you. Everyone's sick. The only difference is our positions."

The man holding the shotgun opened a freezer door, and Senator Fox shoved her inside the freezer. The man with the pistol shot her once through the head, killing her instantly. The man holding the shotgun closed the door.

***

In the back of the bus, Carrie watched Earl open his eyes. "My head is killing me," he said. "Has anyone figured out what's going on yet?"

The fat man with no tongue made unintelligible sounds, and blood started pouring out of his mouth.

Carrie said, "Mommy?"

"What, honey?"

"Will Daddy go to Heaven?"

"Of course he will, honey, when it's time for him to go. Then we'll meet again someday, and we'll all be together forever in God's kingdom of light."

***

Tina followed Leo and Jinx inside the bus.

Jinx removed Earl's handcuffs. Leo released the fat man with no tongue. They forced them from the bus, and then Tina followed them into the hallway of freezers, where Fox and the two gunmen stood waiting.

Earl said, "What the hell's going on here?" The man with the shotgun blew his head off.

Senator Fox examined the fat man, smiling. "Don't damage this one's face," he told the man with the pistol. "I want it to be visible when he's roasting on the spit."

The fat man tried to speak, but his words were unintelligible. The man with the pistol shot him through the heart.

Fox pointed to Earl's headless corpse on the floor. "Put this one in a freezer."

The two gunmen put the corpse in a freezer and closed the door.

Then Fox pointed to the fat man's corpse. "Put him on the spit."

Each gunman grabbed a leg and dragged the corpse toward the ballroom.

***

Tina followed Leo and Jinx to the back of the bus. Only Karen and Carrie remained.

Jinx removed Karen's handcuffs. "Ride's over. It's time to go."

Karen said, "What about Carrie?"

Leo said, "What about her?"

"Can't she come with me?"

"Don't worry," Jinx said. "She'll be right behind you." Then he started dragging her toward the front.

Tina watched Karen turn and take a last look at her daughter. Then she followed Leo and Jinx out of the bus.

In the hallway of freezers, Karen said, "Please don't hurt my daughter."

The man with the shotgun blew her head off.

***

In the back of the bus, Tina stood next to Jinx as Leo removed the little girl's handcuffs.

"Where's Mommy and Daddy?" Carrie said.

Leo cocked his head. "Where do you think?"

A tear rolled down her face. "I think Mommy's in Heaven, but I'm not so sure about my father."

Leo picked her up and carried her out of the bus. Tina followed him and Jinx to the hallway of freezers, where Senator Fox and the two gunmen stood waiting.

Leo set Carrie on the floor. "She's all yours."

"Is that all of them?" Fox said.

Leo nodded. "That's it."

Fox turned to the man holding the pistol. "Kill her."

The man raised his gun to Carrie's head, but then lowered it. "Sorry. I can't do it."

"Why not?"

"She's so young."

Senator Fox shook his head. Then he drew his own gun and blew Carrie's brains out. "Put her in a freezer."

The other man dragged her corpse into a freezer and closed the door.

Leo told Jinx, "Now let's go kill those fucking cops."

Jinx nodded. "Let's do it."

"I need to pee," Tina said, "before we hit the road."

Senator Fox pointed toward the front. "Restrooms are that way."

While crossing the ballroom, Tina saw men in white tuxedoes and women in white ball gowns dancing, talking, laughing, and drinking champagne. A roaming wait staff served cocktails and appetizers throughout. Later, while heading back to the bus, she saw the dead fat man—cleaned, gutted, and with an apple in his mouth—rotating over charcoal in a pig roaster, spinning round and round.

About the Author

Brian Bowyer has been writing stories and music for most of his life. He has lived throughout the United States. He has worked as a janitor, a banker, a bartender, a bouncer, and a bomb maker for a coal-testing laboratory. He currently lives and writes in Ohio. You can contact him at brian.bowyer@hotmail.com.

Turn the page for a bonus short story.

A HAUNTING IN CHICAGO

STORY NOTE: Ever since reading—way back in the 1990s—Poppy Z. Brite's "His Mouth Will Taste of Wormwood" (which is Brite's homage to H. P. Lovecraft's "The Hound"), I had wanted to write an homage. Many years passed. Then I read a story about some dogs . . .

***

"What's your name?" the man said. He wore a huge, nasty-looking (apparently the wound was still bleeding) bandage on his hand, but she thought he was attractive.

"Tamra," she said. "What happened to your hand?"

"I'm Lars. And I slammed it in a car door."

"Sounds painful."

"It was."

"Looks painful, too."

He shrugged. "Yeah, well, the doctor prescribed me some good medication, so I'm not feeling any pain." He sipped his drink. "I'm not supposed to be drinking on the medicine, of course. But you only live once, right?"

She smiled. "Now *that,* Lars, I'm not so sure about."

He laughed.

Tamra thought he sounded a little nervous.

"Can I buy you a drink?" he said.

"Sure."

"What are you drinking?"

She sipped her cocktail. "This is a cosmopolitan."

"Be right back." He walked to the bar.

She watched him order two drinks and bring them to her table.

"Mind if I join you?" he said.

"Be my guest."

***

They ended up back at his place.

Lars had told her that he was thirty (Tamra was twenty-six), but he looked closer to forty. He was obviously successful, however: he lived in a building on Michigan Avenue, with a view of Grant Park from his seventh-floor apartment's kitchen window.

He shared the apartment with a big German Shepherd. "His name is Hugo," Lars said, rubbing Hugo's head. Hugo regarded her quizzically, but his tail wasn't wagging.

"Does he bite?" Tamra said.

"No. It just takes him a while to warm up to new people."

"Do you have any vodka?"

"Of course. Come on. The minibar's in my bedroom."

Tamra followed Lars into his bedroom. Lars closed the door, leaving Hugo out in the hallway. They had a few drinks, and then they made love. Tamra thought the sex was okay, despite the fact that Lars had seemed nervous the whole time—even with the booze and the medication in his system. Afterward, Lars went into the adjoining bathroom.

And then another man spoke to Tamra from a corner of the bedroom: "He will kill you unless you kill him first."

Startled, Tamra—still lying on the bed—turned to look at the man who had spoken. He appeared to be about sixty, and he was completely transparent. He had a full head of gray hair, wore a nice gray suit, and she could see through him all the way to the wall behind him. "Are you a ghost?"

"Yes. I'm Edward. And unless you kill Lars, you'll be just as dead as I am. There's a knife in his nightstand. You have to get it out now. He's going to come out with a rope and ask if he can tie you up. If you let him, you will die. If you don't, he still won't let you leave this place alive. The only way you'll live is if you kill him. I can't stop him, of course, but I *can* control animals, so if you can get to the bedroom door and let the dog in, I may be able to use the dog to assist you. Good luck."

The ghost disappeared before her eyes.

Tamra opened the nightstand and saw a large, vicious-looking knife. *This is madness,* she thought. But she took the knife from the nightstand nevertheless and held it beneath the blanket.

Lars came out of the bathroom still naked, holding a rope. His penis was rising toward another erection. "Mind if I tie you up?"

Tamra—also still naked—sprang from the bed with the knife thrust out in front of her. "Stay away from me!"

Beyond the door, Hugo started barking.

Lars began approaching her. "What the fuck are you doing with my knife?"

Tamra rushed toward the door. "Leave me alone!"

By the time she reached the door, Lars had grabbed a fistful of her hair. She opened the door.

Hugo lunged forward into the room, knocking them off balance.

Both of them spun around and hit the floor. Tamra landed first. Lars landed on top of her. When he did, the blade of the knife pierced his throat all the way to the hilt. He immediately rolled off of her and pulled the knife from his neck, bleeding profusely. He frothed and made a lot of gurgling sounds, and then he died.

Hugo—tail wagging—began licking blood up off the floor.

Tamra watched Edward materialize out of thin air at the foot of the bed. The ghost looked more transparent and less substantial than he had before. "Congratulations," he said. "You saved your own life."

"My buzz is wearing off," Tamra said. "I need a drink."

"Of course," Edward said.

Tamra got up and walked over to the minibar. She grabbed a bottle of vodka and took several drinks from it. Then she looked at herself in the mirror behind the minibar. She was glad that she had been naked when Lars had fallen on the knife. His blood was in her hair, on her face, on her shoulders, and on her chest. "Do you think I should take a shower," Tamra said, "before I call 911?"

"I don't think you should call 911."

"You don't?"

"No. What are you going to tell them? That you stabbed a man in the throat because a ghost told you the man was going to kill you?"

"It was self-defense."

"They'll never believe you. You don't have any wounds—not even a bruise, or a scratch. They'll charge you with first-degree murder. They may even try to say you were involved with the murders of all the bodies they'll find in the room at the end of the hallway."

"What are you talking about?"

Edward gestured toward the bedroom door. "Go see for yourself."

Tamra took a drink. Then, taking the bottle with her, she left the bedroom and walked to a closed door at the end of the hallway.

She opened the door. The large room was full of human skeletons. Skeletons piled on top of skeletons. Probably a hundred at least. Maybe more. As far as she could see, there wasn't a scrap of flesh on any of them. All of the gleaming skeletons looked as if they had been picked clean. Tamra closed the door.

"See what I mean?" Edward said. He was standing right beside her, facing the door. Apparently he could just appear whenever and wherever he wanted to.

"Go take a shower," he said. "I'll take care of the body."

***

Tamra had only been in the shower for maybe two minutes when the need for another drink seized her. She wished that she had just brought the vodka with her into the shower. *I need to get a handle on my drinking,* she thought. *But not tonight. Not after this bullshit.* Leaving the shower running, she stepped out onto one of the towels that she had put down. She dried off a little bit with another towel, and then stepped into the bedroom.

Edward was bent over Lars's corpse. Beams of light were streaming from the corpse into Edward's disembodied form. From the waist down, the corpse was now a skeleton, and Edward was more substantial than he had been before he had begun *(feeding? drinking? absorbing?)* whatever it was that he was doing. He never looked up at Tamra during the process while she crossed the room and grabbed the bottle of vodka.

She took the bottle with her back into the shower.

***

Fifteen minutes later, Tamra staggered out of the shower. She dried off. Then she stumbled into the bedroom.

Lars's corpse had been transformed into a skeleton.

She got dressed. Then she took the bottle with her into the kitchen.

Edward sat at the kitchen table. His legs were crossed. He was still transparent, but he looked more substantial than he had the first time she had seen him. "Did you have a nice shower?"

"I'm drunk," Tamra said. "I think I need to pass out for a while."

"Perhaps you should," Edward said. "We'll talk tomorrow. We have much to discuss."

***

Tamra woke up hoping that most of last night's events had occurred in a dream. That hope burst like a soap bubble, however, when she sat up on Lars's bed and saw his skeleton on the floor. She had passed out fully dressed, and—surprisingly—she hadn't been in blackout. Last night's occurrences were blurry, but she pretty much remembered everything.

From elsewhere in the apartment, she heard the sound of Hugo barking.

"Dog needs out," Edward said. He had materialized and was standing by the bedroom door. "His harness is hanging on a hook in the living room."

Tamra got up and took a drink of vodka. Then she took another one. "Ah," she said. "The miracle of alcohol. This day is looking better already. Okay, I need to pee and brush my teeth, and then I'll take Hugo out."

She went into the bathroom and emptied her bladder. Then she squirted some toothpaste on a finger and brushed her teeth.

When she came back out, Edward was still standing in the bedroom. Tamra took another drink, and then he followed her into the living room.

Hugo stood by the door expectantly, tail wagging. It took her a couple of minutes to get the harness on, but he waited patiently while she figured it out.

"So what do I do?" Tamra said. "Take him to the park?"

Edward shrugged. "If you want. Although I'm pretty sure that Lars simply let him walk around in front of the building."

"Okay," Tamra said. "We'll be back."

They stepped out into the hallway. They rode the elevator down to the lobby. No one spoke to Tamra, and she didn't make eye contact with anyone.

They went outside. The day was warm. The sky was blue.

Hugo did his business. They went back inside.

Edward was in the kitchen when they returned to the seventh-floor apartment. He pointed at the pantry. "His food is in there. He has plenty of treats and chew toys, too."

Hugo—tail wagging—appeared to be looking right at Edward.

"Can he see you?" Tamra said.

Edward smiled. "Oh yes. Hugo can see me. He and I have been friends for about six months now."

Tamra removed Hugo's harness and set it on the kitchen counter. "So who was here first? You or Hugo?"

"I was," Edward said. "I've been in this building for quite some time."

"How long?"

"I don't even know your name."

"Tamra."

"How old are you, Tamra?"

"Twenty-six."

He smiled. "I've been in this building for much longer than you've been alive."

"So you were already haunting this place when Lars moved in?"

"Something like that. But I lived here for a long time before I died, and I've lived here for a long time since.

This is still my place, by the way. I was just permitting Lars to live here, as I've permitted many to live here over the years. Some, of course, ended up staying much longer than others."

"I don't understand."

"I'll explain later. I have a few errands to run."

"Ghosts run errands?"

Edward smiled. "You'd be surprised."

"I need a drink," Tamra said.

"So have a few drinks. And stick around. I'll be back soon with some important news for you. And don't forget to feed Hugo. He's hungry."

***

Tamra passed out for a couple of hours. She woke up around seven o'clock that evening in the living room. Hugo was on the floor, still chewing the rawhide bone she had given him earlier. The bone was almost gone, but there were several more bones in the pantry.

Tamra took a few drinks of vodka. Then she dragged Lars's skeleton out of the master bedroom and put it in the room at the end of the hallway with all the other skeletons. Staring at all those skeletons, Tamra had a hard time believing Lars had killed that many people during the six months he had lived in the apartment. *A victim a day?*

Or every other day? Something like that. And her skeleton would have been added to the collection if not for Edward, so she supposed she needed to at least *thank* the ghost for saving her life.

She took a few drinks of vodka, and then took Hugo outside to do his business. After they came back in, she put fresh food and water in his dishes.

She finished the bottle and opened another one. There were only two more bottles of vodka in the minibar. She would have to go to a liquor store soon.

The ghost showed up around nine o'clock that night. She was seated at the kitchen table, reading a novel on her phone. She looked up and saw that Edward was sitting across from her. She put her phone down. "I never thanked you for saving my life," she said. "So thank you for saving my life."

He smiled. "Tell me about yourself, Tamra."

"What do you want to know?"

"Do you live here in Chicago?"

"No. I live in Elmhurst with my parents."

"Twenty-six and still living with your parents?"

"I just moved back in with them about a month ago. I'm recently divorced."

"So what brought you to Chicago?"

"I've been coming here once a week to see my daughter."

"Your daughter?"

Tamra took a drink. "Yes. Emily. She's six."

"I take it your ex-husband lives in Chicago, and he has custody of your daughter."

"Yes. Nate. He's forty."

"So he's fourteen years older than you. That's quite an age difference."

"Yes. I was eighteen when I met him, and he was thirty-two. I was nineteen when I married him, and twenty when I had Emily."

"I take it that Nate has a lot of money."

"Why do you say that?"

"You're a beautiful woman, and I'm sure you were a beautiful young woman at nineteen. Why else would you marry someone that much older than you unless they had a lot of money?"

Tamra took a drink. "I fell in love with him. But yes, he has a lot of money, and he had a lot of money even then. He was already a hotshot lawyer when I met him, and in retrospect I think the money probably had a lot to do with it. Possibly everything."

"You're obviously an alcoholic," Edward said. "Is that why Nate has custody of your daughter?"

"Of course." Tamra took a drink. The vodka burned and one of her eyes watered. "At the moment, I'm in no condition to raise Emily on my own."

"At least you're not in denial."

"No. I'm long past denial. Actually, I don't think I ever *was* in denial. Not about my alcoholism, anyway. Plus, I don't have much money. That's why I'm living with my parents again. My publisher puts royalties in my account once a month, but trust me, it isn't much. And writers don't get health insurance, of course, so Emily is far better off with Nate right now than she would be with me."

"Was your alcoholism one of the reasons your marriage ended?"

Tamra took a drink. "No. That didn't have anything to do with it. Nate's an alcoholic too, actually. He's a functioning alcoholic. I was a functioning alcoholic, too, for many years, but my drinking has gotten a lot worse since the divorce, since I'm no longer an everyday part of Emily's life. I'm hoping to make enough money off my next book to go to rehab."

"Was Nate mean to you when he drank? Did he abuse you?"

"Oh, no. Nate was a wonderful husband. He's a wonderful father, too."

"Then why did you get divorced?"

Tamra shrugged. "I suppose we just fell out of love with each other. But we're still good friends. We'll always be good friends because of Emily."

"I never had any children myself," Edward said. "The only thing in my life I was ever passionate about was business. And I have a business proposition for you."

"Oh yeah?"

"Yes. I need someone to move into this apartment and take care of things for me from time to time."

Tamra took a drink. "I can't even imagine what rent on this place must be."

"You'd never have to worry about rent or anything else. All of that automatically comes out of an account. All you'd have to do is feed Hugo and take him outside a couple of times a day. I've grown fond of Hugo these past six months."

"That's it?"

"For now, yes. If anything else comes up, I'll let you know."

"You're telling me that I can live in this apartment, on *Michigan Avenue,* free of rent, for feeding Hugo and taking him outside?"

"Yes. And anything else that may come up. I *do* like light, so I'll need you to change lightbulbs whenever they burn out. You'll also be compensated financially, of course. So what do you say? Will you do it? Will you move in here and take care of things for me?"

Tamra took a drink. "Absolutely."

"Excellent," Edward said. "There's a bank card in Lars's wallet. Go get it."

Tamra took a drink. Then she got up and went into the master bedroom.

Lars's clothes were still on the floor where he had left them. She found the wallet in his pants. The name on the card was S. B. Smith.

She took the bank card with her into the kitchen, sat back down, and took a drink.

"I don't know the exact balance," Edward said, "but I'm sure there's enough on that card to last for the rest of your life. Find a pen and paper so I can give you the codes."

Tamra took a drink. "I'll just put them in my phone."

He told her a username, a password, and a PIN number, and she sent all three of those in a text message to herself. Then she went to the bank's website, clicked onto the Online Banking homepage, and logged in. "This can't be right," she said, after she saw the account balance. The dollar amount was staggering. She looked up from her phone, but the ghost was gone.

Hugo stood by the pantry door, staring at her expectantly. His tail was wagging.

Tamra got up and gave him a rawhide bone.

***

The following day, Tamra took a train out to Elmhurst and went to her parents' house. Her parents weren't home, but Scooter—their very old coonhound—lay on the sofa in the living room. He didn't raise his head, but looked up at Tamra and thumped his tail a couple of times when she walked in. Scooter's once-black coat was now mostly gray and white.

She packed a suitcase full of clothes and grabbed her laptop. She left a note for her parents on the kitchen table, saying that she had sold the film rights to one of her novels and that she was moving into an apartment on Michigan Avenue.

Then she headed back to Chicago.

***

Nate brought Emily to the apartment on Saturday morning for a weekend visitation. "Wow!" he said, after Tamra let them in. "This place is amazing! And congrats on the movie deal!"

"Thanks." Tamra sipped her drink. She was drinking a vodka tonic from a cocktail glass rather than straight vodka from a bottle. She had told Nate the same lie that she had told her parents, which she thought they would find more believable than the truth.

And then Emily saw the German Shepherd. "Doggie!" She ran over to him and wrapped her arms around his neck. He sniffed her a couple of times, tail wagging, and then began licking one of her arms.

"He likes you," Tamra said. "His name is Hugo."

"We should have brought Bandit here to play with Hugo!" Emily said.

Bandit was a two-year-old male Labrador-and-Husky mix who was almost the same size as Hugo.

Nate smiled. "Maybe next time."

Hugo followed Emily as the six-year-old took off wandering around the apartment. Tamra wasn't worried about Emily opening the door to the room full of skeletons;

its door was now locked and the key was back in the kitchen drawer where she had found it.

"Again," Nate said, "congratulations. I'll be back tomorrow night to pick her up."

He left.

Tamra found Emily and Hugo in the living room. "Are you hungry?" Tamra said.

Emily nodded. "Yes. Do you have any pizza?"

"No, but I can get some."

"Yay!"

Tamra mixed another drink and ordered a pizza.

***

She didn't see the ghost for about two weeks, and then he materialized in the living room shortly after nine o'clock on a Tuesday morning. Tamra—already drinking vodka—sat on the sofa, writing on her laptop. On the floor at her feet, Hugo chewed on a rawhide bone. Both of them looked up at Edward. He looked more transparent and less substantial than Tamra had ever seen him.

"I have some bad news," he said. "My only other assistant committed suicide last night on Fullerton Avenue."

"Oh no," Tamra said. "I'm sorry to hear that."

Edward nodded. "I had been hoping to have more time to groom you for this position, but now that she's gone, the duty that she performed falls squarely on you."

"Okay," Tamra said. "What do you need me to do?"

"I need you to lure people to this apartment and kill them for me."

"You're joking, right?" Tamra said, but she knew that he wasn't. Suddenly everything about the arrangement made perfect sense.

"No," Edward said. "I'm not joking. Men, women, children—it doesn't matter. The more the better. I just need human bodies, and I need one fast."

She thought of those beams of light streaming from Lars's corpse into Edward's disembodied form, and how much better he had looked afterward compared to how bad he looked now. "What are you?" she said. "Some kind of an energy vampire, or something?"

"I'm someone who needs your help," Edward said.

Tamra finished her drink. Then she closed her laptop and stood up. "I can't help you."

"Sure you can. You're a beautiful woman. You won't have any problems luring people back to this apartment."

Tamra shook her head. "No. I'm not a murderer."

"Have you forgotten the fact that I saved your life?"

"I understand the situation now, Edward! Lars was working for you! Maybe he wanted out. Or maybe you thought I could do a better job. But you just told me yourself that you were grooming me for this position. And I'm not doing it. Hell, it's probably why your assistant committed suicide last night, because she was tired of killing people for you."

"You have two choices, Tamra. You can either kill people for me—and live a long, happy life in this apartment with unlimited wealth while you do it—or you can die. The choice is yours."

"I'm leaving." Tamra headed for the door.

"Wait!"

Tamra turned around.

"You will lose two fingers," Edward said. "Then you will go to the hospital and get stitched up. After that, you will come right back here and talk to me, or you will die."

He disappeared.

Then Hugo attacked her. The force of his lunge sent her to the floor. She landed on her back and he landed on top of her. She raised her arms instinctively to protect her face and heard a snapping sound. It occurred so fast that it was over before she understood what had happened: Hugo had caught her left hand in his mouth and bitten off her ring and pinkie fingers. The pain took a few seconds to arrive. When it did, she screamed.

Hugo—seemingly confused—rose off of her and quickly fled the room.

Tamra got up and swayed on her feet. Blood was fountaining from her hand. She wrapped a towel around it and chugged over half a fifth of vodka, emptying the bottle.

Then she grabbed her laptop and staggered to a nearby hospital.

***

Tamra did not have to wait long in the emergency department's lobby before a nurse led her into an examination room.

A doctor—a Japanese woman—entered the room soon thereafter. She appeared to be exhausted. "What happened?"

"A dog attacked me."

The doctor seemed disinterested and unimpressed. "Do you know if the dog has been vaccinated for rabies?"

"Yes." It was a fairly-confident guess. "The dog isn't rabid."

The doctor shot her up with something for the pain, cleaned her wounds, and stitched them up. Then she gave her some antibiotics, some painkillers, and the name of a surgeon to call later about repairing her mangled hand.

She left, headed west, and staggered to the Lakefront Trail. The sun was shining. She saw a lot of joggers and people walking their dogs. Her hand was starting to throb again, but she was still drunk and it didn't bother her. She needed more vodka, though. She still had several bottles at the apartment, but she had no intention of going back there—even though Edward had told her that she would die if she didn't come back and talk to him after getting her hand stitched up. Besides, he couldn't use Hugo to kill her unless she went back to the apartment, anyway. She was glad she had her laptop with her. It wouldn't bother her at all to leave the rest of her stuff behind. She decided that she would just buy another bottle and then take a train to Elmhurst. She was still filthy rich unless Edward had cancelled the S. B. Smith bank card, and even if he had, there was enough money in her own bank account to last until she figured out what to do.

She turned and started walking north along the trail, rather than south, toward the train station instead of the apartment.

She flinched when the first dog lunged at her. It was a white Pomeranian. It barked, growled, and snapped its jaws at Tamra from the end of its strained leash. "Benji! Stop it!" the surprised owner shouted. "Benji! What the fuck is wrong with you?"

A few steps down the trail, another dog—a border collie—lunged toward Tamra as she approached, barking, growling, and snapping its jaws. Its owner had the same surprised reaction as the Pomeranian's owner. The man, straining to hold the collie back, said, "Stop it, Jasper! What the hell has gotten into you?"

Then a third dog, a fourth, and a fifth—all of them barking, growling, and lunging at Tamra as their owners pulled back on their leashes.

I can control animals, Edward had told her the first time she met him, and she realized through a haze of alcohol and painkillers that his ability wasn't limited to the confines of the apartment. She needed to get out of Chicago, and fast.

She heard a man yell, "Thor! No! Get back here!"

Then Tamra heard a barking deeper than the barking of all the other dogs. She turned around and saw a Rottweiler running straight toward her, its teeth bared, its leash trailing along behind it.

"Thor!"

The owner ran too, but Thor was already way ahead of him.

"Thor! No! Get back here!"

Thor hit Tamra's chest with his front paws and knocked her onto her back. He landed on top of her. She tried to shove him off, but he was too strong.

"Thor! No! Leave her alone!"

She felt the heat of Thor's breath against her face, and then she felt his teeth against her throat.

Edward! Tamra screamed his name inside her mind. *Edward, I'll go back and talk to you!*

Immediately, Thor released her.

And then the owner was there, out of breath and full of apologies. A small crowd had gathered.

Tamra grabbed her laptop and got up. Holding her mangled hand against her chest, she took off running south, headed for the apartment.

***

Edward stood in the living room when she got there. "Welcome home, Tamra. I'm glad you finally came to your senses."

She ignored him and went straight into the kitchen. Hugo stood by the pantry door. His tail started wagging when he saw her.

She set her laptop on the table, opened a bottle of vodka, and took several drinks in a row. Then she turned around and saw that Edward had joined her in the kitchen.

"All of this was so unnecessary," Edward said. "Now we can get on with our business, and you can live a long, happy life."

Tamra took a few more drinks. Then she shook her head. "Not happening."

"What are you talking about?"

"I'd rather die than kill for you. I just wanted to drink some more vodka before I go. So go ahead. Sic Hugo on me again, or whatever it is you do. I'm ready. Otherwise, I'm going back to Elmhurst."

Edward smiled. "Actually, Tamra, that's a good idea."

She took another drink. "What is? Using Hugo to kill me?"

"No. You going back to Elmhurst. Since you're no longer afraid of death, I'll have to find another way to persuade you to work for me, and I know just the way to do it. So go on back to your parents' house. You'll see a message from me when you get there. When you see the message, you will have twenty-four hours to get back here and agree to work for me. Otherwise, your daughter will die."

Tamra took a drink. "I hate you." She took another drink and grabbed her laptop. "You're evil, you're insane, and I hate you."

She left.

***

There was an ambulance and a cop car parked in her parents' driveway when Tamra's cab stopped in front of their house. "Wait here," she told the driver. "I might be going right back to the train station."

She got out and went inside.

Her father was dead. Scooter was dead, too. Their bodies were being tended to.

Her mother sat in the kitchen, crying. "It's the damnedest thing," her mother said. "Scooter was always such a kind, gentle dog. And good lord, he'd gotten so old he could barely move. And then he just attacked your father while he was taking a nap and ripped his throat out for no reason. And then Scooter must have keeled over and died right after he did it. All of this just happened about twenty minutes ago. The ambulance and the police just got here. It makes no sense."

Tamra hugged her mother. "I'm so sorry, Mom. And I hate to run off so quickly at a time like this, but I literally have life-or-death business in the city right now that I have to deal with. I just had to stop by here and get some papers from my room."

"Oh, honey, that's okay. There's nothing you or anyone else can do for your father now, anyway."

"Are you going to be okay, Mom?"

"Yes, honey. I'll be okay. I'll call you with the funeral arrangements and everything."

"Okay, Mom. I'll be back as soon as I can. I love you."

"I love you too."

Tamra left and headed back to Chicago.

***

"Nice place," Russell said, after following Tamra into the living room. She had only met him in a club about an hour ago, and he had agreed to leave the club and walk her back to her apartment. He seemed like a nice guy. She hated that she was going to have to kill him, but she had decided that she would do whatever was necessary to protect her daughter's life.

Hugo stood in the doorway to the kitchen. His tail wasn't wagging.

"Pretty dog," Russell said.

"His name is Hugo," Tamra said. "Come on. The minibar's in my bedroom."

Russell followed her into the master bedroom.

Tamra was staggering—despite the fact that it was only about eight o'clock at night. She had been drinking vodka and taking painkillers all day long, and now she was having a hard time keeping her eyes open. When Russell had asked about her bandaged hand, she had told him she slammed it in a car door.

She stumbled over to the minibar and just stood there, swaying on her feet.

"Are you sure you should be drinking?" Russell said. "You look like you're about to pass out."

"Probably not. I think I need to rest for a little bit. Will you be mad?"

"Of course not." Russell helped her to the bed.

"Stick around," Tamra said. "I won't sleep long, and then we'll have a lot of fun together."

Russell nodded. "You bet."

Less than a minute later, Tamra was unconscious.

***

Russell went to the minibar and poured a glass of whiskey. When he turned around, he saw a ghost. He sipped his whiskey.

The ghost said, "You don't look at all surprised to see me."

"I'm not," Russell said. "I've been seeing ghosts my entire life."

"Do you like this apartment?"

"Of course."

"Do you like money?"

"Yes, I do."

The ghost smiled. "I'm Edward, and I have a business proposition for you."

Russell sipped his whiskey. "I'm listening."

***

Tamra woke up. Her hand was throbbing. She sat up.

Russell was sitting up next to her on the bed, staring at his phone. "Feel better?"

"I don't know yet." She put two painkillers in her mouth and swallowed them with vodka. Then she looked at her phone to check the time: 11:07 p.m. She had slept for about three hours.

Tamra got up and went into the bathroom. She brushed her teeth, emptied her bladder, and washed her hands.

Then she grabbed some handcuffs from beneath the sink and returned to the bedroom.

Russell saw the handcuffs, but didn't say anything. He finished his drink and stood up.

Tamra's phone rang. She looked at the screen: Nate was calling her.

"My ex-husband," she told Russell. "He only calls if it's something about our daughter."

She pressed the TALK button. "Hello?"

"Emily's dead!" Nate shrieked, crying hysterically. "Bandit killed her! Our beautiful daughter is dead!"

Tamra felt something inside of her die.

Then Russell shoved a blade into her neck to the hilt and yanked it to the left.

Printed in Great Britain
by Amazon

60610856R00087